TO THE LIONS

A TALE OF THE EARLY CHRISTIANS

ALFRED J. CHURCH

EONN PUBLISHING

CONTENTS

1. An Accusation	1
2. An Old Story	8
3. A Christian Household	17
4. Love Or Duty?	23
5. A Plot	31
6. Pliny And The Christians	39
7. The Arrest	47
8. Before The Governor	54
9. Rhoda's Evidence	64
10. The Examination	70
11. The House Of Lucilius	78
12. A Martyr's Testimony	85
13. A Discovery	92
14. A Letter From Trajan	102
15. The Amphitheatre	108
16. "The Christians To The Lions"	115
17. Escape	123

1

AN ACCUSATION

THE time is the early morning of an April day in the year of Our Lord 112. So early is it that the dawn has scarcely yet begun to show in the eastern sky. The place is a burial-ground in the outskirts of Nicæa, one of the chief towns of the Roman province of Bithynia. We must imagine an oblong building, about sixty feet in length and forty in breadth. The roof is arched, and at the highest point, perhaps twenty feet from the ground. The further end from the door is semi-circular, like what is called an apse in church architecture. There are four windows in each of the side walls; these, however are not glazed, but furnished with wooden blinds, which can be opened or shut as the weather serves. The building is commonly lighted with lamps, six of which hang from the roof. It has little ornament about it; the floor is tessellated, but the work is rough; the little cubes of which the pattern is made are of baked clay, not stone or marble, which are more expensive materials; and the patterns themselves are rude and carelessly worked. The walls are of rough stone, plastered and colour-washed. The semicircular end only is hung, to a distance of about six feet from the ground, with purple curtains.

Such was a Christian church in the early part of the second century.

It must not be supposed that even this simple building had been erected for its own use by the Christian community. Even if it could have found the means to do so, it would not have ventured so to attract public attention. For the Christian faith was not one of the religions which were sanctioned by the State; and it existed only by sufferance, or rather, we might even say, by stealth.

This meeting-house of the Christians of Nicæa was really the club-house of the wool-combers of that city. The wool-combers' guild or company had, for some reason, passed to other places. Old members had died, and few or no new members had been admitted. Much of its property had been lost by the dishonesty of a treasurer. Finally the few surviving members had been glad to let the building to persons who were acting for the Christian community. No questions were asked as to the purpose for which it was to be used; but, as two or three out of the half-dozen of surviving wool-combers were Christians, it was well understood what this purpose was. It would have been, by the way, more exact to say "a burial club." This was the object for which it had been founded. Its social meetings had been funeral feasts; hence its situation in the near neighbourhood of a cemetery. This made it particularly suitable for meetings of the Christians. Assemblies held before dawn—for this was the custom—and close to a burial-ground, would be little likely to be observed.

The congregation may have numbered one hundred persons, of whom at least two-thirds were men. There was a division between the sexes—that is to say, the men occupied all the seats (benches of the plainest kind) on one side of the building, and the front half of those on the other. It was easy to see that, with a very few exceptions, they were of humble rank. Many, indeed, were slaves. These wore frocks reaching down to the knees, cut square at the neck, and for the convenience of leaving the working arm free, having one sleeve only. These frocks were made of coarse black or brown serge, trimmed at the bottom with sheepskin. Two or three were sailors, clad in garments so coarse as almost to look like mats. Among the few worshippers of superior station was an aged man, who wore a dress then rarely seen, the Roman toga. The narrow purple stripe with which it was edged, and the gold ring which he wore on the forefinger of his left hand, showed that he was a knight. His order included, as is well known, the chief capitalists of Rome, and, among other speculations, was accustomed to farm the taxes. Titus Antistius—this was the old man's name—had been the agent for this purpose in Bithynia, but he had for some time retired from the occupation. His age, his blameless character, and the wealth which he dispensed with a liberal hand, helped, together with his rank, to make him the principal character in the Christian community of Nicæa. He sat on a cushioned chair, but the privilege had been conceded to him quite as much on account of his age and infirmity as of his social position.

The only other member of the congregation whom it was necessary to mention was an elderly man who sat immediately behind Antistius. His dress, of plain but good material, showed that he belonged to the middle class. His name was Caius Verus.

The semicircular end of the building was reserved for the clergy, of whom three were present. They wore the usual dress of the free citizen of the time, a sleeved tunic, with a cape over the shoulders that reached to the waist. The only thing that distinguished them from the congregation was that their dress was wholly white. One of the three was an old man; his two colleagues were middle-aged. The three sat facing the people, with a plain table used for the Holy Supper in front of them. On either side of the apse, as we may call it, on the line which divided it from the main body of the building, were two reading desks. On each a volume was laid. One of these volumes contained the Old Testament, in the Greek version of the Septuagint, the other the New.

The minister left his seat behind the Table, and advanced to address the people. It was evident that his agitation was great; indeed, it was some time before he could command his voice sufficiently to speak.

"Brothers and sisters," he said, "I have a grave and lamentable matter to lay before you. Serious charges have been brought against our brother Verus—for brother I will yet call him. It has been alleged against him that he has gambled, and that he has sacrificed to idols. Caius Verus," he went on, "answer as one who stands in the presence of God and His angels. Do you know the house of the merchant Sosicles?"

Verus stood up in his place. Whatever he may have felt about the truth of the charges and the likelihood of their being proved, he did not lose his confident air. He had stood not once or twice only in his life in positions of greater peril than this, and he would not allow himself to be terrified now.

"I know it," said the accused, "as far as a man may know a house which he enters only for purposes of business. I have had dealings with Sosicles on account of the Church, as the brethren know. He is a heathen, but a man of substance and credit; and the moneys of the Church have increased in his hand."

"It is true," said the minister; "and I have often wished that it could be otherwise. But the holy Apostle Paul tells us that if we would have no dealings with such men, we must needs go out of the world. But you affirm that you have not companied with him as with a friend?"

"I affirm it."

"Cleon, come forth!" said the minister to a young man who was sitting on one of the back benches.

Cleon was a slave from the highlands of Phrygia—not a Greek, but with the tinge of Greek manners, which had reached by this time to all but the most inaccessible parts of Lesser Asia. He was a newcomer. Verus scanned his face narrowly, but apparently without any result.

"Tell your story," said the minister; "and speak without any fear of man."

Cleon went on in somewhat broken Greek. It is a month since I came into the possession of the merchant Sosicles. He bought me of the heir of the widow Areté, of Smyrna. She had provided in her will that I should be free; but her heir disputed it, and the Proconsul gave judgment against me." The poor lad choked down a sob as he said this, and a thrill of sympathy ran through his audience. "Sosicles knew that I was a Christian, and took two hundred drachmæ from the price for that reason. I heard him say that Christians had scruples and were obstinate. I worked chiefly in the garden; but about a week since I had to take the place of Lycus, the cup-bearer. The master had flogged him so severely for stealing a flagon of Chian wine that he could not stand. When I came into the dining-chamber the dishes had been removed. I mixed the first bowl, and set it on the table before Sosicles. I filled the cups out of it. Sosicles poured out a libation. 'To Apollo and Aphrodite,' he said. I filled the other cups. There were eight guests in all. They all said the same words, excepting Verus, who lay on the host's right hand. I observed that he drank without speaking. When I saw this, I thought to myself that he must be a Christian; and then I remembered that I had seen him here. The drinking went on. I filled the cups many times. Towards the end of the first watch, Sosicles, who by this time was, as I should judge, half-tipsy, poured out a libation to Hermes. He said to Verus: 'This toast you shall not refuse. For Apollo and his harp you care not; no, nor for Aphrodite with her girdle of love; but Hermes, with his money-bags, is your true god.' Verus laughed, and said nothing. Then Sosicles grew angry. I had heard that he was apt to be quarrelsome in his cups. 'By Hercules,' he said, 'you shall drink it! I will have no dealings with atheists. Drink it, or we close our accounts.' Verus tried to put him off; but it was of no use—Sosicles only grew the more furious. At last I heard Verus mutter the words. About the middle of the second watch I came in again. Some of the guests had gone away; others were asleep. My master and Verus were playing at dice. Each had a pile of money before him. I watched them for a time, and it seemed to me that my master scarcely knew what he was doing. About half an hour afterwards Verus went home. I noticed that he had a bag of money with him. It seemed heavy. He was quite sober."

Self-possessed as he was, the accused could not quite hide the dismay with which he listened to this narrative. He had not noticed the new cup-bearer at Sosicles' entertainment. He had often heard his host say that he would have no Christian slaves: they were troublesome, and made difficulties about doing what they were told.

Accordingly, he had made sure that he was safe. He would gladly have escaped saying the idolatrous words. His Christian belief, without being sincere, was yet strong enough to make him shrink from committing so manifest an offence against it. Of love for Christ he had nothing; but he certainly feared Him a great deal more than he feared Hermes. Still, when he came to balance his scruples against the present loss of breaking with his host, they were found the lighter of the two. So he had come to speak the words; but he had followed them up with a sentence muttered under his breath: "Who, for all that, is a false demon." With this he had salved his conscience, which by this time had come to heal of its wounds with a dangerous ease.

Now he rapidly reviewed his position, and thought that he saw a way of escape. He spoke with an appearance of moderation and candour that did credit to his power of acting.

"I have a fault to confess, but it is not the grievous sin of which Cleon accuses me. It is true that I was at Sosicles' banquet. I repent me of having concealed this from the brethren. But it is not true that I spoke the blasphemous words. What I said was a colourable imitation of them, intended to appease the unreasonable rage of a tipsy man. Who knows what trouble might have arisen—not to me only, but to the whole community—if I had angered him? As for the dice-playing, I played, indeed; but I played to humour him. I so contrived it that he won back the greater part of what he had lost. If I gained anything, I gave the whole of it to the poor. As for the bag of money which Cleon saw me carry away, it was given to me in payment of an account. These things I confess, because I would not hide any thing from my brethren, and desire to make any amends that they may judge to be fitting. Yet there is something that I would urge. Does not the holy Apostle command that an accusation be not believed against an elder except from two or three witnesses? If I am not an elder, yet the Church has put me in a place of trust. Were I standing on my trial before the unbeliever, would he condemn me on the testimony of a single slave?"

"Take heed what you say," interrupted the minister. "In this house there is neither bond nor free."

"It is so," said Verus. "I spoke after the fashion of the world. But who is this young man? Is he not a stranger, known to you only by a letter which he brought from the elders of Smyrna? Can you condemn me for aught beyond that which I have myself willingly owned on his single testimony?"

He looked round on the congregation as he spoke, and saw that his appeal had not been without its effect. It was true that, as the minister had said, all in that house were equal; but the difference between slave and free man was too deeply ingrained into human nature in those days to be easily forgotten. And no one felt it more than the slaves themselves. It was they who would have been most shocked to see a respectable merchant found guilty on the single evidence of one of their own class. A murmur of approval ran round the congregation; and when the minister put the question, though some did not vote either way, the general voice was for acquittal.

Before the minister could speak, the old knight rose in his place.

2
___

AN OLD STORY

VERUS bent on the old man the same closely scrutinising look with which he had regarded the slave. Again he failed, it seemed, to connect the face with any recollections in his mind. There was, as we shall see, a dark past in his life which he was most unwilling to have dragged into the light. But he had no reason to associate Antistius with it, and nothing more than a vague sense of distrust haunted him, but he felt that if the old man had anything to say against him, he would be a far more formidable witness than the young Phrygian slave.

"You have been in Rome?" said the knight to Verus.

"Yes," he answered; "but not for some years past."

"Nor I," went on the old man; "nor do I want ever to see it again. She is the mother of harlots, drunken with the blood of the saints, and with the blood of the martyrs of Jesus! But when I left it last, seventeen years ago, I carried away with me a memorial of a deed that I shall never forget, nor you either, if there is any thing human in you."

The speaker produced from the folds of his toga a small packet wrapped in a cover of silk. Unwrapping it with reverent care, he brought out a handkerchief stained nearly all over of a dull brownish red.

"Know you this?" he said to Verus.

"Why do you ask me? What have I to do with it?" answered the man, with a certain insolence in his tone. The majority in his favour made him confident.

"Yet you should know it, for it is a blood that was shed by your hands, though the blow was dealt by the axes of Cæsar. If seventeen years are enough to make you forget the martyr Flavius, yet there are those who remember him."

It is impossible to describe the effect which these words produced. In those days of peril, next to his love for his God and Saviour, the strongest emotion in a Christian's heart was his reverence for the martyrs. They were the champions who had fought and fallen for his faith, for all that he held dearest and most precious. He could not, he thought, reverence too much their patience and their courage. Were these not the virtues which he might at any hour be himself called on to exercise.

This reverence had, of course, its meaner counterpart in a base and cowardly nature such as Verus'. The man had not belief enough to make him honest and pure; but he had enough to give him many moments of agonizing fear. It was such a fear that overpowered him now. Any wrongdoer might tremble when thus confronted with the visible, palpable relic of a crime which he believed to be unknown or forgotten. But this was no ordinary wickedness. The betrayer of a martyr was looked upon with a horror equal to the reverence which attached itself to his victim.

Nor was it only the scorn and hatred of his fellow-men that he had to dread. There were awful stories on the men's lips of informers and traitors who had been overtaken by a vengeance more terrible than any that human hands could inflict; and these crowded upon the wretched creature's recollection. His face could not have shown a more overpowering fear had the pit itself opened before him. The staring eyes, the forehead and cheeks turned to a ghastly paleness and dabbled with cold drops of sweat, proved a terror that in itself was almost punishment enough.

But the criminal was almost forgotten in the thrill of admiring awe that went through the whole assembly. With one impulse men and women surged up to the place where the old knight was standing with the venerable relic in his hand. To see it close, if it might be to press their lips to it, was their one desire. The old man was nearly swept off his feet by the rush. The minister stepped forward, and took him within the sanctuary at the end of the meeting- house. The habit of reverence kept the people from pressing beyond the line which separated it from the body of the building, and they were partially satisfied when the handkerchief was held up for their gaze.

When silence and quiet had been restored, Antistius told his story.

"I went to Rome in the last year of Domitian's reign. It was at the season of the holiday of Saturn, which as some of you know, the heathen in Italy keep in the month of December. But it was no holiday time in Rome. The Emperor was mad with suspicious rage, and no man's life was safe for an hour; and the higher the place, the greater the danger. Yet there was one whom, though he was near to the throne, every one thought to be safe. This was Flavius Clemens. He was the Emperor's cousin: his sons were the next heirs to the throne. He was the gentlest, the least ambitious of men. It is true that he was a Christian, and the Emperor's rage at the time burned more fiercely against the Christians than against any one else; but the Emperor knew it, had known it for years, and had made him Consul in spite of it.

"When I reached Rome, he was near the end of his year of office. I dined with him on the Ides of December, for he was an old friend, and he told me—for we were alone—how he looked forward to being rid of his honours. 'Only eighteen days more,' he said, 'and I shall be free!" Ah! he spoke the truth, but he little thought how the freedom was to come. He told me, I remember, what an anxious time his Consulship had been. The Consul, you see, has to see many things, and even do many things, which a Christian would gladly avoid. To sit at the theatre, to look on at the horrid butchery of the games, to be present at the public sacrifices, these are the things which a man can hardly do without sin.

" 'But', he said, 'my good cousin, the Emperor, has considered me. Happily he has been my colleague, and he has taken a hundred duties off my hands, which would have been a grievous burden on me.' And then he went to tell me of some troubles which had arisen in the Church. A certain Verus had the charge of the pensions paid to the widows, and of other funds devoted to the service of the poor, and he had embezzled a large part of them. 'You see,' he went on, 'we are helpless. We cannot appeal to the courts, as we have no standing before them; in fact, our witnesses would not dare to come forward. For a man to own himself a Christian would be certain death; and though one is ready for death if it comes, we must not go to meet it. So, whether we will or no, we must deal gently with this Verus.' And he did deal gently with him. Of course, he had to be dismissed; but he was not even asked to repay what he had taken—Flavius positively paid the whole of the deficiency out of his own pocket. And he spoke in the kindest way, I know, to the wretch, hoped that it would be a lesson to him, begged him to be an honest man in the future, and even offered to lend him money to start in business with.

"And yet the fellow laid an information against him with the Emperor! It would not have been enough to charge him with being a Christian; he was accused of witchcraft, and of laying plots against the Emperor's life. He used to mention Domitian's name in his prayers, for he was his kinsman as well as his emperor, and they got some wretched slave to swear that he heard him mutter incantations and curses. And Domitian, who was mad with fear—as he well might be, considering all the innocent blood that he had shed—believed it.

"I shall never forget what I saw in the senate-house that day. It was the last day of the year, and Flavius was to resign his office. There sat Domitian with that dreadful face, a face of the colour of blood, with such a savage scowl as I never saw before or since. Flavius took the oath that he had done the duties of his office with good faith, and then came down from his chair of office.

"In the common course of things the senate would have been adjourned at once. But that day the Emperor stood up. What a shudder ran through the assembly! Every one saw that the tale of victims for that year was not yet told. The question was, whose name was to be added? Domitian called on Regulus, a wretch who had grown gray in the trade of the informer. He rose in his place. 'I accuse Flavius Clemens, ex-consul, of treason,' he said. Why should I weary you, my brethren, with the wretched tale? To name a man in those days was to condemn him. I have heard it said by men who have crossed the deserts of the South that if a beast drops sick or weary on the road, in a moment the vultures are seen flocking to it from every quarter of the sky. Before, not one could be seen; but scarce is the dying beast stretched on the sand, but the air is black with their wings. So it was then. One day a man might seem not to have an enemy; let him be accused, and on the morrow they might be numbered by scores.

"Flavius, as I have said, was the gentlest, kindest, most blameless of men. But had he been the worst criminal in Rome, witnesses could not have been found more easily to testify against him. They brought in that wretched slave with his story of muttered incantations.

"You will say, perhaps, 'But he could not bear witness against his master!' Ah! my friends, they had a device to meet that difficulty. They sold him first, and, mark you, without his master's consent, to the State. Then he could give evidence, and the law not be broken. Then this villain Verus came forward. He told the same story, and with this addition, that he had been bribed to keep the secret, and he brought out the letter in which Flavius had offered him the money, as I have told you. Kind as ever, the Consul had written thus: 'We will bury this matter in silence. Meanwhile you shall not want means for your future support. Flaccus the banker shall pay you 100,000 sesterces [about £1,000].'

"Then senator after senator rose and repeated something that they had heard him say, or had heard said of him—for no evidence was refused in that court. At last one Opimius stood up. 'Lord Cæsar,' he said, 'and Conscript Fathers, of the chief of the crimes of Flavius no mention has been made. I accuse him of the detestable superstition of the Christians.'

" 'Answer for yourself,' said the Emperor, turning to the accused.

"He stood up. Commonly, I was told, he was a faltering speaker, but that day his words came clear and without hindrance. We know, my brethren, Who was speaking by his lips. He spoke briefly and disdainfully of the other charges, utterly breaking down the evidence, as any other court on earth but that would have held. Then he went on, 'But as to what Opimius has called "the detestable superstition of the Christians," I confess it, affirming at the same time that this same superstition has made me more loyal to all duties, public or private, of a citizen of Rome. I appeal to Cæsar, who hath known me from my boyhood, as one kinsman knows another, and who, being aware of my belief, conferred upon me this dignity of the Consulship, which is next only to his own majesty. I appeal to Cæsar whether this be not so.'

"He turned to Domitian as he spoke. That unchanging flush upon the tyrant's face fortified him, as I have heard it said, against shame. But he kept his eyes fixed upon the ground, and for a while he was silent. Then he said, 'I leave the case of Flavius Clemens to the judgment of the fathers.'

"You will ask, 'Did no one rise to speak for him?' I did see one half-rise from his seat. They told me afterwards that it was one Cornelius Tacitus, a famous writer, but his friends that were sitting by caught his gown and dragged him back, and he was silent. And indeed, speech would have served no purpose but to involve him in the ruin of the accused.

"Then the Emperor spoke again, 'We postpone this matter till tomorrow.' Then turning to the lictors—

"'Lictors,' he said, 'conduct Flavius Clemens to his home. See that you have him ready to produce when he shall be required of you.'

"This, you will understand, was what was counted mercy in those days. A man not condemned was allowed the opportunity of putting an end to his own life. That saved his property for his family. In the evening I went to Flavius's house. He was surrounded by kinsfolk and friends. With one voice they were urging him to kill himself. Even his wife—she was not a Christian, you should know—joined her entreaties to theirs. Perhaps she thought of the money, and it was hard to choose beggary instead of wealth; certainly she thought of the disgrace. Were she and her children to be the widow and orphans of a criminal or an ex-consul?

"He never wavered for an instant. 'When my Lord offers me the crown of martyrdom,' he said, 'shall I put it from me?' That was his one answer; and though before he had been always yielding and weak of will, he did not flinch a hair's-breadth from this purpose.

"That night, I was told, he slept as calmly as a child. The next day he was taken again to the Senate, and condemned. But I heard that at least half of the senators had the grace to absent themselves. One favour the Emperor granted to him, as a kinsman; he might choose the manner and place of his death. He chose death by beheading, and the third milestone on the road to Ostia. It was then and there that the holy Apostle Paul had suffered; and Paul, whom he had heard in his youth, was his father in the faith. I saw him die; and besides his memory, that handkerchief, stained with his blood, is all that remains to me of him."

"What answer you to these charges?" said the minister to Verus.

He said nothing; and his silence itself was a confession.

Still it would have ill become the Church to act in haste. Antistius was asked to give proofs of the identity of the Verus who was present that day with the Verus who had brought about the death of Clemens. The old man told how his suspicions had been first aroused; how a number of circumstances, trifling in themselves had turned this suspicion into certainty. And he then indicated, though only in outline, his discoveries—that Verus had been following again the same dishonest practices that had brought him into disgrace at Rome. He promised that he would bring the evidence in detail before the Church at some future time.

The accused was still silent.

Then the minister addressed him:—"Verus, you have heard what has been witnessed against you. We do not repent that you were acquitted of the first charges. Be they true or no—and what we have since heard inclines us to believe them—they were not rightly proved. God forbid that the Church should be less scrupulous of justice than the tribunals of the unbeliever; but to the accusations of Antistius you yourself oppose no denial. Therefore hear the sentence of the Church.

"I have thought whether, after the example of the holy Apostle Paul, I should deliver you over to Satan for the destruction of the flesh. I do not doubt either of my power or of your guilt; yet I shrink from such severity. Therefore I simply sever you from the Communion of the Church. Repent of your sin, for God gives you, in His mercy, a place for repentance. Make restitution for aught in which you have wronged your brethren, or them that are without. And now depart!"

The congregation left a wide space, as if to avoid even the chance of touching the garment of the guilty man, as he hurried, with his head bent downwards to the door.

When he had gone, the minister addressed the congregation.

"Brothers and sisters," he said, "I cannot doubt but that we shall be soon called to resist unto blood. There are signs that grow plainer every day, that the rulers of this world are gathering themselves together against Christ and His Church. It was but yesterday that I received certain news of that of which we had before heard rumours, to wit, that the holy Ignatius of Antioch suffered at Rome, being thrown to the wild beasts by command of the Emperor. But the fury that begins at Rome spreads ever into the provinces, and it cannot be hoped that we shall escape. We have this day made an enemy, for assuredly Caius Verus will not forget the disgrace that he has suffered, but will betray us, even as Judas betrayed his Lord. Therefore it becomes us to be ready. Provoke not the danger, lest your pride go before a fall. Many a time have they that were over-bold and presumptuous failed in the time of peril, and so have sinned against their own souls and done dishonour to the name of Christ. So far, therefore, as lieth in you, study to be quiet; and assuredly, when the time of need shall come, you will not be the less bold to confess Him who died for you. More I will say, if the Lord permit, when the occasion comes. Should it seem dangerous to meet in this place, I will summon those with whom I would speak to my own home."

Some words of advice about smaller matters connected with the management of the Church affairs followed this address. He then pronounced a blessing, and the congregation dispersed.

3

A CHRISTIAN HOUSEHOLD

WE will follow one party of worshipers to their own home, a farmhouse lying about a mile further from the city than the chapel which has just been described. This party consists of four persons, a husband and wife, and two daughters.

The head of this little family is a man who may perhaps count seventy summers. But though seventy years commonly mean much more in the East than they do in our more temperate climate, he shows few signs of age, beyond the white hair, itself long and abundant, which may be seen under his broad-brimmed hat. His tread is firm, his figure erect, his cheek ruddy with health, his eyes full of fire; yet he had seen much service, of one kind or another, during these threescore years and ten. Bion, for that was the veteran's name, was a Syrian by birth. He had followed Antiochus, son of the tributary king who ruled part of Northern Syria under the Romans, to the siege of Jerusalem. A more hot-headed, hare-brained pair than the young prince and his favourite aide-de-camp could not have been found. They laughed to scorn the caution of the Romans in attacking the great city by regular approaches. "We will show you the way in," said the prince to the centurion who showed him the works.

Of course this effort failed. If success had been possible in this way the Romans would have achieved it long before. Scarcely a third of the Syrian contingent came back alive from the forlorn hope to which they had been led. Bion was one of the survivors, but he was desperately wounded, and had not recovered in time to take part in the final assault. He did not lose, indeed, either pay or promotion. Before he was five-and-twenty he was commander-in- chief of the army which the Syrian king was permitted to maintain.

This was a sufficiently dignified post, and his pay, coming as it did from what was notoriously the best furnished treasury in Asia, was ample. He might have been satisfied, if he had been content to be a show soldier. But he was not content; and unfortunately, now that the turbulent Jews had been quieted, it seemed, for good, there appeared no chance of being anything else. His restless spirit led him into intrigues with the Parthians: a compromising letter fell into the hands of the Roman Governor, and he had barely time to escape across the Euphrates. The Parthians, with whom he now took service, gave him fighting enough with the wild tribes who were perpetually trespassing over their northern and eastern borders.

Again his reckless valour brought him promotion; and his promotion brought him enemies. An arrow which certainly could not have come from any but his own men, missed him only by a hair's-breadth; two nights afterwards, the cords of his tent were cut, and he narrowly escaped the dagger which was driven several times through the canvas before he could extricate himself from the ruins; and it was nothing but a vague feeling of suspicion, for which he could not account, that kept him from draining a wine-cup which had been poisoned for his benefit. These were hints that it was well to take. He left the camp without saying a word to any one, and made the best of his way out of Parthia.

The difficulty was where to go. The world in those days consisted of Parthia and Rome, and he was not safe in either. Nothing was left for him, he thought, but becoming a brigand; and a brigand he accordingly became. It was a perilous profession, for the Roman governors of Asia kept a strict look-out, and did not approve of any one plundering the provincials but themselves. One band after another that he joined was broken up, and at last he bound himself to one in the neighbourhood of Ephesus. His chief here was a young man of singular beauty, and of a fine, generous temper who had been driven into this lawless life by the oppression of the Roman officials. Bion, who was by some years his senior, formed a great friendship for him, and the two contrived to keep their rough followers in as good order as was possible in a band of brigands.

And now came the strange incident that was to change the course of Bion's future life. The two were watching the road that ran from Ephesus across the heights of Mount Tmolus to Smyrna for a tax-gatherer who was expected to come that way with his money-bags. It was not long before a solitary rider could be seen, slowly making his way along the steep road which wound up the wooded mountain side. The companions rushed from their hiding-place, and in a few moments were at his side. Bion seized the bridle of his mule, and the chief called upon him to give up all the money that he had with him. The rider, whose figure and face were concealed by a traveller's cloak and cape, answered in a voice of singular sweetness, "Silver and gold have I none, but what I have I give thee." At the same time he threw aside his disguise. If the brigand chief had seen a grinning skull instead of the sweet and loving face, with eyes full of compassion and tenderness, bent upon him, he could not have been more startled. He turned to fly.

The rider dismounted with an agility which no one would have expected from so old a man, followed him, and caught him by the cloak. "Listen to me, my son," he said. "Four years since, I left you in the charge of Polydorus of Smyrna. At the end of two years, when I had finished my visiting of the churches of Asia, I went to Smyrna. They told me that you had left the city. Some said that you had fled to the mountains, and were living by robbing. I went to Polydorus. I said to him, 'Where is the treasure that I left in your hands?' He did not know what I meant. 'You left no treasure in my hands,' he said. 'I left a treasure which the Lord himself had committed to me,' I answered, 'even the soul of the young man Eucrates.'

"Then I went out to seek you. For if I had trusted it to an unfaithful steward, I should have myself to answer for it to my Lord. But now, thanks to our Father and His Christ, I have found it again. And you, my son, will surely not take it from me."

This good shepherd, who had thus sought and found his wandering sheep upon the hills, was the Apostle St. John. The persuasiveness of this constraining love was such as no one could resist. Before he had finished his appeal the young man was sobbing at his feet. The three returned to Ephesus together, for Bion would not leave his friend. He too had been touched by some power that he did not understand, that seemed to dwell in the old man's words.

The Apostle was a man of no small influence in Ephesus. His character was of that rare sweetness and beauty which even the world is constrained to love. And with this love a certain awe was mingled. It was rumoured that a Divine protection guarded him from danger. Had he not been thrown into a caldron of burning oil and come out unhurt? Hence he was able with little difficulty to obtain from the Roman governor of the province an amnesty for his two companions, and even to get for Eucrates restitution of the property which had been taken from him. The young man did not forget Bion, but made him the tenant and afterwards the purchaser of a farm which he owned in the neighbourhood of Nicæa.

Meanwhile Bion had been listening with a heart disposed to conviction to the instructions of St. John. It was the late autumn when he had given up his brigand's life, and he was among the candidates who presented themselves for baptism at the Whitsuntide of the following year.

No more devout and earnest soul was to be found among the converts than Bion. The fiery temper which he shared with the teacher who had brought him to Christ was tamed rather than broken. He had found, too, during his sojourn at Ephesus, earthly happiness as well as heavenly peace.

One of the most trusted lay-helpers of the Church was a devout centurion, who had served under Titus at the siege of Jerusalem. Bion recognised in him, not without a smile at his own foolish boastfulness in times past, the very officer who had been appointed to attend on his master, and who had afterwards helped to nurse him during his tedious recovery. The old comrades were glad to meet again.

But Bion found in Manilius' house a more powerful attraction than friendship. This was the centurion's adopted daughter, Rhoda. Manilius had found her, then a girl of some seven years old, in a burning house on that terrible day when the Holy City was destroyed. Her father, mortally wounded in the last desperate struggle which his countrymen had waged against the Roman storming parties, had crawled back to his home, and the child, made old beyond her years by the dreadful experiences of those months of siege, was sitting by the dying man, striving in vain to staunch the flow of blood from his wounds.

Anxiety for his child mastered the Jew's hatred of foreigners. In broken Latin he besought Manilius to be good to his daughter. It was a strange responsibility for a lazy and somewhat reckless soldier, but it seemed to sober him in an instant. He found his Tribune, and obtained permission to take his young charge to the camp. From thence she was transferred as soon as possible to the house of a merchant of his acquaintance at Cæsarea.

No spoil that he could have carried off from the sack of Jerusalem could have proved such a treasure to him as the little Rhoda. She had learnt from her Christian mother, who, happily for herself, had passed to her rest just before Jerusalem was finally invested, some Gospel truths, and Manilius listened with attention which he might not have given to an older teacher when she told him in her childish prattle the story of the life and death of Jesus.

When the rewards for services in the great siege were distributed, he received a permanent appointment at Ephesus. Here he came under the influence of St. John, and here he, his wife, and the little Rhoda were received into the Christian community.

Rhoda was now a beautiful young woman of two-and-twenty; but no suitor had hitherto touched her heart. Bion, in the full strength of his matured manhood, for he was now close upon the borders of forty, with the double romance of his strange conversion and his old life of adventure, took it by storm. The lovers were married on the day after his baptism, and took possession of the Bithynian farm before the end of the year.

Rhoda's story has been given in the story of her husband. She was a woman of a character gentle yet firm, who never seemed to assert herself, whom a casual observer might even suppose to be of a yielding temper, but who was absolutely inflexible when any question of right or wrong, or of the faith which she clung to with a passionate earnestness of conviction was concerned.

The two girls, Rhoda and Cleoné, were singularly alike in figure and face, and singularly different in character. They were twins, and they had all the mutual affection, one might almost say, the identity of feeling, which is sometimes seen, a sight as beautiful as it is strange, in those who are so related. Rhoda was the elder, and the ruling spirit of the two. This superior strength of will might be traced by a shrewd observer in the girl's face. To a casual glance the sisters seemed so exactly alike as to defy distinction. But those who knew them well never confounded them together. The dark chestnut hair and violet eyes, rare beauties under that Southern sky, the delicately rounded cheeks, with their wild-rose tinge of colour, the line of forehead and exquisitely chiselled nose, modified by the faintest curve from the severely straight classical outline, were to be seen in both. But Rhoda's lips were firmly compressed; Cleoné's were parted in a faint smile; and the gaze of Rhoda's eyes had a directness which her sister's never showed. Rhoda's nature was of the stuff of which saints are made; Cleoné's was rather that which gives peace and sunshine to happy homes. Hitherto the quiet in which the two lives had been passed had given little to occasion anything like a divergence of will. In the small questions that occurred in daily affairs Cleoné had followed without hesitation the lead of her sister. A time was now at hand which was to apply to their affection and to Rhoda's influence a severe test.

4

LOVE OR DUTY?

THE two sisters, Rhoda and Cleoné, did not lack admirers. Maidens so fair and gracious would have attracted suitors even had they been portionless. But it was well known that they would bring handsome dowries with them, for Bion's farm had prospered under his hands, while Bion's wife had inherited the savings which her adopting father, the centurion Manilius, had made from his pay and prize-money.

But Rhoda's admirers found it impossible to get beyond admiration. In those early days of Christianity there were no vows of celibacy for men or women; though, indeed, the feelings and thoughts that led to them were rapidly growing up. Yet no cloistered nun of after times could have been more absolutely shut out from all thoughts of love and marriage than this daughter of a Bithynian farmer. She did not affect anything like seclusion, or seek to stand aloof from the business and even the little pleasures of daily life. She took her part in the work of the farm. No fingers milked the cows or made the butter more deftly than hers. In the harvest field she would follow the reapers, and bind the sheaves more untiringly and more skillfully than any, except Cleoné. When the vintage came round, and the purple and amber grapes were plucked by the women for the men to tread in the vats, no one filled her baskets more quickly than Rhoda. And if a weakly calf, or lamb, or an early brood of chickens, hatched before the frosts were fairly gone, wanted care, there was no one who could give it so efficiently and tenderly as Rhoda. In fact, it was her vocation from her cradle to serve others. Every good woman has such a vocation in her degree, but some embrace it with a devotion that leaves no room for any personal ties. Rhoda was one of these rare souls; and the boldest lover soon found that she was not for him, and, indeed, had no care for any earthly suit. She never needed to repulse an admirer. A very short time sufficed to show that she was absolutely unapproachable; and she went untroubled on her way, followed by something of the awe which might be felt for an angel come down from heaven.

It was natural, of course, that her first thought should be to serve the community of believers to which she belonged. And there was a way in which this desire could be fulfilled. The early church had the practice, lately revived among ourselves, of calling devout women to the office of deaconess, and of thus making a regular use of their zeal. The need of such helpers in the ministry was especially great when the Greek habits of life prevailed, and women were in a large measure secluded from society. They wanted helpers and advisers of their own sex who might go where men would not have been admitted. Such a helper the Church of Cenchreæ, the busy port of Corinth, had at an earlier time in Phœbe, whom St. Paul commends so kindly to his fellow Christians at Rome. This was the office to which Rhoda inclined. It was her youth only that hindered her admission to it. Though no vows were demanded, still there was a natural feeling that those who put their hands to such a work should not go back from it, and the presiding minister of the Christian community hesitated about giving this regular call to one so young and so beautiful as Rhoda. Bion too, and his wife, though they would not offer a direct opposition to their daughter's wish, were not sorry to see its full accomplishment postponed. They were too good people to grudge her to the service of Christ and His Church; yet they could not help shrinking from all that this vocation seemed to mean. In any case it could hardly fail to take her much from their family life. Nor could they hide from themselves that, if troublous times should come, if the persecution which was always possible, and even probable, should begin, the first victims would be those who held office in the Church.

Next to her own feeling of devotion, Rhoda's strongest desire was to make her sister a sharer in her work. Nothing could have made her draw back, but the thought of not having Cleoné by her side was inexpressibly painful to her, and she banished it with all the force of her resolute will. Her best and truest course would have been to recognise the difference between her sister and herself, of which, indeed, she could not fail to have some knowledge, to acknowledge that Cleoné was made for the duties of happiness and home, and to crush down all the feelings and wishes in her heart that helped to hide this from her. But, in common with many great natures, she had, to use a common phrase, the defects of her good qualities. She said to herself, "I am called to serve my Lord; this service is the highest aim in life, the most perfect happiness that I can enjoy, and what can I do better for the sister who is like a part of my soul than to bring her to share in it? Shall I not be doing well if I can bring two hearts instead of one to Him?"

Cleoné would have yielded with scarcely a struggle to the strong will of her sister—for she was in her way not less devout—if it had not been for another influence. She had found among her suitors one to whose affections her own went out in answer.

Clitus was a Greek, an Athenian by birth, who had come to Bithynia in the train of Pliny, the Roman Governor. He had been a remarkably successful student in the University of Athens. He had been chosen, though then only a junior, to give the complimentary address with which the City of the Muses welcomed a visit from Pliny, as a distinguished Roman man of letters; and his pure Attic style and manly delivery had attracted the visitor's notice. He had been no less successful as an athlete than he was as a learner in the school of philosophy and rhetoric. No competitor could throw him in the wrestling ring or outstrip him in the foot-race. The crew captained by him had won for three years in succession—an unparalleled distinction—the prize in the boat-races in the Bay of Salamis. In the midst of these triumphs he was struck with a sudden sense of the vanity of the pursuits to which he had been devoting himself. A fellow-student, a friendly rival, who had been only less successful than himself in study and sport, had been carried off by a violent fever. He was a stranger from Ephesus, and, as none of his kindred were at hand, Clitus, as his nearest friend, had the sad duty assigned to him of putting the torch to the funeral pile on which the body was to be consumed, and of gathering the ashes for the urn which was to be placed in the family sepulchre at Ephesus. The most brilliant rhetorician that the University contained had been chosen to speak the funeral oration. Clitus listened to him with the closest attention, for he eagerly desired some word of comfort and hope. The speaker was a disciple of a well-known school, which asserted nothing and questioned everything. As long as he spoke of the dead man, of his virtues and his achievements, nothing could be better than his language, so full was it of tenderness and grace; but when he came to treat of the future, he failed. He could only disparage or doubt the beliefs of others. He ridiculed the popular faith, the gloomy pit of Tartarus, the shining fields of Elysium. He reviewed the speculations of philosophers only to express his dissatisfaction. But his chief scorn was for a doctrine which he said had been proclaimed not far from the place where they were standing, some sixty years before. "It was a Jew," he said, "who had the boldness to propound these absurdities in this city of philosophers; nor was he a man without culture. I have heard it said by one who listened to him that, though his accent was detestable, he quoted from our poets. But his teaching was sheer frenzy. Every man was to rise from his grave! Mark you, every man! Criminals, slaves, barbarians—did you ever hear of such madness?" And then the speaker went on to propound his own theory, which, by the way, was amazingly like some that are being thrust upon us now. "Men will survive in their race. The individual perishes; but if he had done anything for his fellows, has been a poet, or an orator, or an inventor, he lives in the greatness of what he has done, and in the fame which waits upon it."

Clitus turned away in profound discontent. Then it occurred to him, "Can I find what I want elsewhere? There is Bion the Golden-Mouth lecturing at Ephesus. Perhaps he has something more satisfying to tell me." To Ephesus he went. But there Clitus heard nothing more than he had heard at Athens. Yet his visit was not fruitless. One day, when his restless thoughts drew him from his bed before sunrise, he fell in with a little company of men and women who were making their way through the half-lighted street. He followed them, entered with them a building in the outskirts of the city, and listened to a discourse on the subject of the very doctrine which he had heard ridiculed at Athens. "Then," he said to himself, "this wild fancy still holds its ground!" He came again and again. What he heard interested him deeply, and when he came to make acquaintance with some of his fellow-hearers, he found that, humble mechanics or slaves as they were, they had a wonderful elevation of thought, and even of language. Meanwhile, it was necessary to find some employment. Just at that time the younger Pliny came to Ephesus, on his way to take possession of his government in Bithynia, and Clitus attended his levée. Pliny, always glad to surround himself with educated men, offered employment as a secretary, and Clitus accompanied him to his province. It was thus that he became acquainted with the little community that worshipped in the guild-house of the wool-combers of Nicæa, with the household of Bion, and with the beautiful Cleoné. An opportunity had occurred of serving Bion in some matter that brought him into the Proconsul's court, and the acquaintance had grown into intimacy. Clitus was now a catechumen, or person under instruction, and it was intended that he should be baptized at Whitsuntide.

In the afternoon of the day following the assembly described in the first chapter, the young Roman had found his way to the farm by help of one of the excuses which lovers are never at a loss to invent. Possibly it was not an accident that his coming was timed for an hour at which Rhoda would be busy with some errand of mercy, for Rhoda viewed the young man as a formidable opponent, and, for all her unworldliness, was clever enough to prevent any private interview between him and her sister. The elder Rhoda was busy with her household cares; Cleoné was helping her father in the vineyard. He was pruning—a delicate task, which he was unwilling to trust to any hands but his own; she followed him along the rows, tying up to their supports the shoots which were left to bear the vintage of the year. It was here that Clitus found her, and as Bion was inclined to favour his suit, no place could have suited him better. If we listen awhile to their talk, we shall see how matters stood between them. Clitus was in high spirits.

"Give me joy, Cleoné," he said; "the letter from the Emperor arrived this morning, and it grants the Governor's request. I am to have the Roman citizenship; and now everything is open to me."

The girl could not refuse her sympathies to his manifest delight; but her mind was somewhat sad, and it was with a forced gaiety that she answered, "Well, my lord—for you will soon be one of the lords of us poor provincials—how shall we speak to you? What Roman name shall you be pleased to adopt? Shall you be a Julius Cæsar or a Tullius Cicero?"

"To you, Cleoné," said the young man, "I shall always be Clitus, the name under which I had the happiness to know you. But, seriously, the Governor is kind enough to let me take his own family name, and I shall be Quintus Cæcilius."

"And when do you leave us for Rome?" said the girl, giving all her attention, it seemed, to binding up a refractory shoot.

"Leave you? for Rome? I said nothing about leaving."

"But the career—in this poor place there is nothing to satisfy you. You said that all things were now open to you, and where are 'all things' to be found, but at Rome?"

"You misunderstand me—you wrong me, Cleoné. I have no such ambition as you seem to think. I desire nothing better than to spend the rest of my days here, if I can but find here the thing that I want. I did but mean that no road by which I may find it well to travel will be shut to me when I am a citizen of Rome. But be sure that the road, whatever it is, will never take me very far from Nicæa."

The girl was silent. She had seen from the first, with a woman's quick apprehension of such things, that there was a serious purpose in the young Greek's manner, and she had tried, as women will try, even when they are not face to face with such perplexities as were troubling poor Cleoné, to put off the crisis.

Clitus went on: "I am to have the government business as a notary in the province. The Governor promises that other things will follow. But I am afraid this does not interest you."

"I am sure," answered the girl, "we all feel the greatest interest in you."

"But you, Cleoné, you!" cried the young man, and he caught her hand in his as he spoke. "You know that this is my ambition: to have something which I can ask you to share. I came to tell you that it seems to be within my reach, and you ask me when I am going to Rome! Oh! it is cruel; and when I have been hoping all the time that there might be something to work for."

Poor Cleoné was in a sad strait. The struggle between love and duty is often a hard one; but at least the issue is clear, and a loyal heart crushes down its pain, and chooses the better course. But here there seemed to be love on both sides, and duty on both sides. Which was she to choose? She knew that Clitus loved her, and though she had never looked quite closely and steadfastly into her own heart, she felt that she loved him. And he was worthy, too. Any woman might be proud of him. Why should she not do as her mother had done before her, and give herself to a good man who loved her? There was love and there was duty here. But then, on the other side, there was the Church, its claim upon her, the work that lay ready for her hand—and Rhoda, who was her second self, from whom she had never had a thought apart, whose love had been the better half of her life ever since she could remember anything. It was a sore perplexity in which she was entangled.

She stood silent. But her silence was eloquent. Clitus, though he was no confident lover, saw that it was not her indifference that he had to fear. If he had been no more to her than other men, she could easily have found words—kind, doubtless, but plain and decisive enough—in which to bid him go. She had even left her hand in his.

She was scarcely conscious of it, so full was her mind of the struggle; but consciousness would have come quickly enough if his touch had been repugnant to her.

At last she spoke: "Oh, Clitus, this is not a time for such things as you talk of. Remember what the elder said the other day. There is danger at hand, and we must be ready to meet it. Would it be right to hamper ourselves with things of this world? Does not the holy Apostle Paul tell that they who marry——"

She paused, blushing crimson when she remembered that her lover, though his meaning was plain enough, had not gone as far as speaking of marriage.

"Ah! if you were only my wife," cried Clitus, "I should fear nothing.

"Has he not said," she went on, "that they who marry shall have trouble in the flesh? And, when I might be comforting and strengthening others, to have to think of myself! O, Clitus, I feel that I am called to other things. Rhoda and I are not as other women; she tells me so, and she is always right. I could not go against her."

Perhaps it was as well that just at that moment, Bion, who had finished his work for the time among the vines, advanced with outstretched hands to greet the guest. It was a relief to both to have the interruption.

5

A PLOT

ON the evening of the day when Clitus and Cleoné held their conversation among the vines, as described in the last chapter, another conversation, which was to have no little influence on their fate, was going on. The place was a wine-shop, kept by a certain Theron, in the outskirts of Nicæa, and not far from the Christian meeting-house. Theron's customers were, for the most part, of the artisan class. But he kept a room reserved for his few patrons that were of a higher rank. In this room three persons were sitting at a citron-wood table, one of the innkeeper's most cherished possessions, which only favoured customers were permitted to see uncovered. A flagon, which could not have held less than two gallons stood in the middle of the table. It was about half full of the potent wine from Mount Tmolus, mixed, however, with about half its bulk of water. From this flagon each guest ladled out the liquid into his own drinking-cup.

One of the three is already known to us. This is Verus, the unworthy member whose banishment from the Christian community has been described. The second, to whom, it may be observed, his companions pay a certain respect, is an elderly man, in the ordinary dress of a well-to-do merchant. There is a certain air of intelligence in his face. But the keen, hungry look of the eyes, the pinched nose, the thin, bloodless lips, tightly closed, but sometimes parting in a smile that never reaches the eyes, give it a sinister look. Lucilius—for this was his name—was a man of good birth and education, but he had given up all his thoughts to money-making, and the tyrant passion had set the mark of his servitude on his face.

The third is a professional soothsayer or fortune-teller. The fortune- teller of to-day commonly exercises his art by means of a pack of cards, while he sometimes consults a tattered book of dreams, or even professes to gather his knowledge of the future from the motions of the planets. Cards were not then invented; dream-interpreting and star-reading were not held in very great repute. Our soothsayer practised the curious art of discovering the future by the signs that might be discerned in the entrails of animals. My readers would think it tedious were I to give them the details of this system. Let it suffice to say that the liver was held to carry most meaning in its appearance. If the proper top to it were wanting, something terrible was sure to happen. There were lines of life in it, and lines of wealth. Each of the four "fibres" into which it was divided had its own province. From this you could discern perils by water, from that perils by fire; a third warned you of losses in business, a fourth gave you hopes of a legacy. This was the art, then, which the third of the three guests professed. He called himself Arruns, but this was not his real name. Arruns is Etruscan, whilst the man was a Sicilian, who, after trying almost everything for a livelihood, had settled down as an haruspex in Nicæa. But the Etruscans were famous over all the Roman world as the inventors of the soothsaying art, and professors of it found an Etruscan name as useful as singers sometimes find one that is borrowed from Italy, or French teachers a supposed birthplace in Paris. Arruns, if he had little of the Etruscan about him in his language, which was Latin of the rudest kind, spoken in a broad Greek accent, had at least the corpulence for which the foretellers of the future were proverbial. His small dull eyes, sometimes lit up with a little spark of greed or cunning, his thick sensual lips, and heavy bloated cheeks, flushed with habitual potations, showed how the animal predominated in him.

He was now holding forth on his grievances in a loud, harsh voice, which he did not forget to refresh with frequent draughts of Tmolian wine.

"It is monstrous, this neglect of the gods! It must bring a curse upon the country. There will be nothing left sacred soon. Who can suppose that if men do not care for the gods, they will go on caring for each other? Children will not honour their parents, nor parents love their children. The sanctity of marriage, the rights of property, everything will disappear, if these atheists are suffered to go unpunished, while they spread abroad their pernicious doctrines."

"Your zeal does you credit," interrupted Lucilius, with a slight cynical smile. "But we all know that Arruns is careful of all that concerns the sacredness of the home."

Arruns was a notoriously ill-conducted fellow, whose life was a scandal to the better behaved, not to say the more pious of the heathen. His wife had long since left him in disgust, and was supporting herself as a nurse. His children he had turned out of doors. The shaft did not wound him very deeply, but he took the hint and became more practical.

"Look at the temples," he went on; "the court-yards are grass-grown. Day after day not a worshipper comes near them. To see smoke going from the altars is as rare as to see snow in summer. And when a man does bring a beast, 'tis some paltry, half-starved creature: a scabby sheep, or a worn-out bullock from the plough, which are not good enough for the butcher's knife, let alone the priest's hatchet. And as often as not, when there is a decent sacrifice, they do not call me in. They grudge me my ten drachmas—for I have had to cut down the fee to ten. 'What should a calf or a sheep's liver have to tell us about the future?' they say. What monstrous impiety! What a flagrant contradiction of all history! Did not Galba's haruspex, on the very day of his death, warn him that he was in danger from an intimate friend? and did not Otho, who was such a friend, kill him within two hours afterwards?"

"Yes," said Lucilius, a little peremptorily, "we know all about these examples and instances. But go on to your own grievances."

"Well, to put the matter plainly, it is simple starvation to me. Twice, thrice last week I had to live on beans and bread. Ten years ago there did not a day pass without two or three sacrifices. I had my pick of good things—beef, mutton, lamb, veal, pork, every day; and now I am positively thankful for a rank piece of goat's flesh, that once I would not have given to my slave. Oh! it is awful; there must be a judgment from the gods on such impiety."

"One would hardly think, from your looks, my Arruns," said Lucilius, "that things were quite so bad as you say. But, tell me, what do you suppose to be the cause of this impious neglect of the gods, and this indifference to the future?"

"The Christians, of course," said Arruns; "the Christians."

"But," interrupted Lucilius, "they can be scarcely numerous enough to make much difference, and I am told that they are mostly poor people, and even slaves; so that they could hardly, in any case, be clients of yours."

"My good lord," said Arruns, "it is not so much the Christians themselves; it is the example they set. People say to themselves: 'These seem to be very decent, honest sort of fellows; they never murder or rob; they are very kind to the sick and poor; we can always be safe in having dealings with them; and they seem to be tolerably prosperous too. And yet they never go inside a temple, nor offer so much as a lamb to the gods.' What could be worse than that? They do ten times more harm than if they were so many murderers and thieves. A good citizen who neglects the gods is a most mischievous person. There is sure to be a number of people who imitate him so far. It is the Christians who are at the bottom of all this trouble."

"But what do you want me to do?" said Lucilius. "Grant that what you say is true, still I see no reason for interfering. I have two or three tenants who are said to be Christians, and they are honest and industrious fellows who always pay me my rent to the day. Why should I trouble them?"

"Pardon me, sir," interrupted Verus, who had as yet taken no part in the conversation. "Pardon me if I remind you that there is something more to be said. The association of the Christians is an unlawful society."

"Of course it is," cried Lucilius; "we all know that; though you, my dear Verus, seem to have been a long time finding it out, if, as I understand, you have been acting as their treasurer."

"I have but lately discovered their true character," said Verus. "When I did, I hastened to leave them."

"Ah!" said Lucilius, with a sneer, "that must have been at the very time when they examined your accounts. Do you know that people have been saying that they, too, made some discoveries?"

Verus, who would have given a great deal to be able to stab the speaker, forced his features into a sickly smile. "You are pleased to jest, honourable sir," he said. "But these Christians are not quite so insignificant or so poor as you think. There is the old knight, Antistius. No one would suppose that he was a rich man. He drinks wine that cannot cost more than a denarius a gallon, and very little of that; but we know what he gives away in alms. It is not only here that he gives. His money goes to Smyrna, to Ephesus, and positively to Rome. You may rely upon this, because it used to pass through my hands."

"And stick there sometimes, I have heard," retorted the other, whose passion for saying bitter things was sometimes too strong for his prudence, and even for his avarice. "But what does that matter to me? What do I care for the way in which an old fool and his money are parted? It does not concern me if he feeds all the beggars and cripples in the Empire."

"You forget sir," returned Verus, "that if Antistius is convicted of belonging to an unlawful society—and there can be no doubt that the community of Christians is such a society—his goods are confiscated to the Emperor's purse, and that those who assist the cause of justice will have their share."

There was a sudden change in Lucilius's careless, supercilious manner, though he did his best not to seem too eager.

"Ah!" he said, "there may be something in that, though I should not particularly like a business of that kind."

"Don't suppose, sir," went on Verus, "that there are not others besides Antistius. There are plenty who are worth looking after. Bion the farmer is wealthy, though one would hardly think it. And there are others who are entangled in this business. You would hardly believe me, if I were to tell you their names. And then it is not only here, it is all through the province that you may find them. I have all the threads in my hand, and I could make a very pretty unravelling if I chose."

"What, then, do you propose?" asked Lucilius.

"That we should lay information to the Governor."

"Will he act? He is all for being philosophic and tolerant."

"He cannot choose but act. The Emperor's orders are stringent. He is very strict about these secret societies. Did you not hear about the fire-brigade that the people of Nicomedia wanted to have? They were nearly ruined by the fire last December. Nothing was ready: not a bucket nor a yard of hose; and when some things were got together, then there was nobody to work. The consequence was that more than half the city, and all the finest buildings in it, were burnt. The people wanted to have a fire-brigade, and the Governor wrote to the Emperor, recommending that the request should be granted. But no. Trajan would not have anything of the kind. If it was not a secret society, it might be turned into one, he said in his letter. No; if we once set the thing going, the Governor must act, whether he like it or no. We must send in as many informations as we can. There will be one from you, and another from Arruns here, who can back it up if he likes with his complaint about the sacrifices. Then there is Theron, our host here, who complains that the Christians are so sober that they are taking the bread out of the tavern-keepers' mouths. As for myself, perhaps my name had better not appear. I should not like to be seen acting against old friends and employers. But it does not much matter who signs them, or, indeed, whether they are signed or not. As long as there are plenty of them, it will be enough; and your secretary can see to that."

At Verus's suggestion, Theron, the innkeeper, was called into the council. He, of course, had a very bad opinion of the Christians.

"They are a very poor, mean-spirited lot," he said; "if they had their way there would not be a tavern open in the Empire. I never see one of them inside my doors. Sometimes, when I have a late company here, I have seen them on their way to their meeting-place, one of the guildhouses in the cemetery here. They are a shabby lot, for the most part—half of them slaves, I should think. I suspect an out-door man of my own of being one of them. He never drinks, or gambles, or fights. I always suspect there is something wrong with a young fellow when he goes on like that. Yes, I should very much like to see the whole business put a stop to. If it is not, the world will soon be no place for an honest man to live in."

A plan of action was agreed upon. A number of memorials were to be presented to the Governor, praying him to interfere with a certain unlawful society, bearing the name of Christians, or followers of Jesus, that was accustomed to meet in the neighborhood of Nicæa. Lucilius, Verus, and Arruns were each to send in such a document, and were to get others sent in by their friends. A number of anonymous memorials in various handwritings were also to be prepared. The more there were, the more likely was the Governor to be impressed.

When the party was separating, Arruns tried to do a little stroke of business on his own account. "This is an important undertaking," he said, in his most professional tone, to Lucilius. "Don't you think that it would be well to consult the gods?"

"My Arruns," said Lucilius, who had no idea of spending his money in any such way, "when I make an offering, I prefer that it should be a thank- offering. When we have done something, I shall not be ungrateful."

The soothsayer was not going to let himself be baffled. If he could get nothing out of the cupidity of Lucilius, he might be more successful in working on the fears of Verus.

"It would have an excellent effect, my dear Verus," he said, "if people could see some proof of your piety. They know that you have been mixed up with these Christians, and they don't all know that you have come out from among them. If there should be anything like a rising of the people—there was one in Galatia the other day, and half a dozen of these impious creatures were torn to pieces before the Governor's guard could interfere—there might be some awkward mistake. We should have plenty of people protesting that they had never been Christians at all, or had left off being so, and you might not be believed, particularly if you had anything to lose. Now, if you were to offer a sacrifice, you would be perfectly safe. No one would dare to wag his tongue against you."

Verus, who, if he had not learnt to believe Christianity, must have at least learned thoroughly to disbelieve the whole Pagan system, heard the suggestion with very little fervour, but felt too uneasy about his position to reject it. He knew that he had compromised himself, and that the danger which Arruns had pictured was not completely imaginary.

"There may be something in what you suggest," he said, after a pause. "Perhaps a lamb to Jupiter or Apollo——"

"A lamb!" interrupted Arruns, who was not disposed to be satisfied with so paltry an offering. "A lamb! The whole country would cry shame upon you. It ought to be nothing less than a hecatomb."

"A hecatomb!" cried Verus, "what are you talking about? Am I the Emperor, that you should suggest such a thing?"

"Well," returned the other, "a hecatomb might, perhaps, be a little ostentatious for a man in your position. But I assure you that nothing less than a 'swine, sheep, and bull' sacrifice would be acceptable. It must be something a little out of the common, for yours is not a common case."

"Well, let it be so," said Verus, "only it must be done cheaply. No gilding of the bulls horns or expensive flowers; I really cannot afford it."

"Leave it to me," answered Arruns. "I will spare your pocket."

With this they separated, the soothsayer chuckling over his success, and the prospect of a plenty which he had not enjoyed for some months, Verus ruefully calculating how many gold pieces the three animals, with the ornaments and the temple fees, would cost him.

6

PLINY AND THE CHRISTIANS

CAIUS PLINIUS CAECILIUS SECUNDUS, commonly known to posterity as the Younger Pliny, has just finished his day's work as Proprætor—that is to say, Governor—of the Roman province of Bithynia. It has evidently worn him out almost to the verge of exhaustion. He has, indeed, the look of feeble health. His gentle, delicate features are drawn as with habitual pain; his cheeks are pale, with just one spot of hectic colour in the middle; the lines on his forehead are deeper than befits his age, for he is but in his forty-seventh or forty-eighth year; his figure is bent and frail, and thin almost to emaciation.

The room shows evident signs of the occupation of a man of culture. Though it is his official apartment, and he has his study elsewhere, it has something of the look of a library. A little bookcase, elegantly made of ivory and ebony, stands close to his official chair. Half a dozen rolls—for such were the volumes of those days—are within reach of his hand. He can refresh himself with a few minutes' reading of on or other of them, when the tedium of his official duties becomes more than he can bear; using a writer's privilege, we can see that Homer is one of the six, and Virgil another. The wall facing him is covered with a huge map of the province; and most of the available space elsewhere is occupied with documents, plans of public buildings, and other matters relating to the details of government; but room has been found for busts of eminent writers, for some tasteful little pieces of Corinthian ware, and for two or three statuettes of Parian marble. At a table in the corner a secretary is busy with his pen; but were we to look over his shoulder we should see that he is not occupied with the answer to a petition or with a report to the Emperor, but with the fair copy of a poem which the Governor has found time to dictate to him in the course of the day.

Pliny has just risen from his seat, after swallowing a cordial which his body physician has concocted for him, when the soldier who kept the door announced a visitor—"Cornelius Tacitus, for his Excellency the Governor." Pliny received the new-comer, who, indeed, had been his guest for several days, with enthusiasm.

"You were never more welcome, my Tacitus," he cried. "Either I am in worse trim for business than usual, or the business of the day has been extraordinarily tiresome. In the first place, everything that they do here seems to be blundered over. In one town they build an aqueduct at the cost of I don't know how many millions of sesterces, and one of the arches tumbles down. Then, in Nicæa here, they have been spending millions more on a theatre, and, lo and behold ! the walls begin to sink and crack, for the wise people have laid the foundation in a marsh. Then everybody seems to want something. The number of people, for instance, who want to be made Roman citizens is beyond belief. If Rome were empty, we could almost people it again with them. But, after all, these things need not trouble me very much. One only has to be firm and say 'No!' But here is a more serious matter, upon which I should like to have your advice."

The Governor handed to his friend two or three small parchment rolls, which he took from a greater number that were lying upon a table. As Tacitus read them, his look became grave, and even troubled.

"What am I to do in this matter?" said the Governor, after a short pause. "For the last two or three days these things have been positively crowding in upon me. You don't see there more than half that I have had. They all run in the same style: I could fancy that a good many are in the same handwriting. 'The most excellent Governor is hereby informed that there is a secret society, calling itself by the name of Christus, that holds illegal meetings in the neighbourhood of this city; that the members thereof are guilty of many offences against the majesty of the Emperor, as well as of impiety to the gods;' and then there follows a long list of names of these same members. Some of these names I recognize, and, curiously enough, there is not one against which I know any harm. Can you tell me anything about this secret society which calls itself by the name of Christus?"

"Yes," answered Tacitus; "it is more than fifty years ago since I first heard of them, and I have always watched them with a good deal of interest since. It was in the eleventh year of Nero—you could only have been an infant then, but it was the time when more than half of Rome was burnt down."

"I remember it," interrupted Pliny, "though I was only three years old; but one does not forget being woke up in the middle of the night because the house was on fire, as I was."

Tacitus went on: "Well, I shall never forget that dreadful time. The fire was bad enough, but the horrors that followed were worse. People, you know, began to whisper that the Emperor himself had had the city set on fire, because he wanted to build it again on a better plan. Whether he did it or not, he was capable of it; and it is certain that he behaved as if he were delighted with what had happened, looking on at the fire, for instance, and singing some silly verses of his own about the burning of Troy. Well, the people began to murmur in an ominous way—you see, more than half of them were homeless. So the monster found it convenient to throw the blame on some one else, and he threw it upon the Christians. You know what a Roman mob is; as long as it has its victims, it does not much care about the rights and wrongs of a case. I did not see much of what was done to these poor wretches, but I saw enough to make me shudder to this day when I go by the place. It was at a corner of the Gardens on the Palatine. They had fastened one of the miserable creatures to a stake, and piled up a quantity of combustibles about him, but not near enough to kill him at once when they were set on fire. I shall never forget his face. It was night, but I could see it plainly in the light of the flames, which yet had not begun to scorch it. There was not a trace of fear on it. He might have been a bridegroom. Boy as I was, it struck me very much, and I said to myself, 'These are strangely obstinate people, I take it, and might be very dangerous to the State.' And that is the view I have always taken of them; and it has been borne out by everything that I have seen or heard."

"But," said the Governor, "have you ever made out that there is anything wicked or harmful in this superstition of theirs? I have heard strange stories of their doings: that they mix the blood of children with their sacrifices, that they indulge in disgraceful licence, and so forth. Do you believe that there is anything in these reports?"

"To speak frankly," replied Tacitus, "I do not. On the contrary, I believe that they are a singularly innocent and harmless set of people; that they neither murder nor steal; and that if all the world were like them our guards and soldiers would have very little to do."

"Yet," said Plinius, "you seem to speak of them in a somewhat hostile tone. If they are so blameless they cannot fail to be good citizens."

"No, this is precisely what they are not," was Tacitus' answer after a few moments' pause. "I take it that obedience is the foundation of our commonwealth, obedience to the Emperor now, as it once was to the Senate and people. No man must set his own will or his own belief above obedience. If he does, he takes away the foundation. Tell one of these Christians to throw a pinch of incense on an alter, and he will refuse. Not the Emperor himself could make him do it. The pinch of incense may be nothing. Neither the State nor any single soul in it may be one whit the worse for its not being thrown; but it is an intolerable thing that any citizen should take it upon himself to say whether he will or will not do it. Depend upon it, my dear Pliny, these Christians, though they never trouble our courts, civil or criminal, are very dangerous people, and either the Empire must put them down, or they will put the Empire down."

"What, then, would you have me do?" asked the Governor.

"Act with energy; arrest these people; stamp the whole thing out."

"But it is too horrible. It is—if you will allow me to say it—it is even absurd. Here are thieves and cut-throats without number at large; profligates who spend their whole lives in doing mischief, and villains of every kind. Yet a Governor is to leave these hawks and kites to themselves, and pounce down upon a flock of innocent doves. Forgive me if I say, my dear Tacitus, that I never saw you so little like a philosopher."

"There are times," replied Tacitus, "when one has to think, not about philosophy, but about policy. Look at the Emperor. You know what manner of man he is. He is not a madman, like Nero; he is not a monster, like Domitian, who was so fond of killing that he could not spare even the flies. But Nero and Domitian were not so stern with the Christians as he is. 'Obey me,' he says, 'or suffer for it. If I let you choose your own way, the Empire falls to pieces.' Yes, my dear Pliny, distasteful as it must be to be a man of your sensibility, you must act."

"I shall consult the Emperor," said the Governor, who felt himself hard pressed by his friend's arguments.

"Certainly," said Tacitus; "it would be well to do so. I understand that he wishes to be consulted about everything; though how he contrives to get through his business is beyond my understanding. But meanwhile act. You need not do any thing final, but Trajan, if I know him, would be much displeased if he were to find that you had done nothing."

"What would you advise, then?"

"Send a guard of soldiers, and arrest the whole company at one of their meetings. It would be easy to learn the place and the time. These societies have always some one among them to betray their secrets; though, indeed, this can hardly be a secret. You need not keep them all in custody. Probably many will be slaves. I hear that the slaves everywhere are deeply infected with the superstition. You can let them go, and make their masters answerable for them. Nor should I take much heed of artisans and labourers; but you will keep any person of consequence that there may be, and, above all, their priests, or elders, or rulers, or whatever they call them."

The Governor pressed a handbell that stood on the table at his elbow, and bade the attendant who answered the summons send for the centurion on duty.

In the course of a few minutes this officer appeared.

"Fabius," said Pliny, "you have heard, I suppose, of certain people that call themselves Christians?"

"Yes, my lord," answered the centurion, "I have heard of them."

It required all the composure—one might almost say the stolidity of look—that is one of the results of a soldier's discipline, to enable Fabius to reply without showing any change of countenance. He had been for some months a "catechumen"—one, that is, who was receiving instruction preparatory for baptism. He had been somewhat inclined of late to draw back. The new faith attracted him as much as ever, but there were difficulties which it put in his way. Could he hold it and be a soldier? His teachers differed. The eldest minister, a man of liberal views, thought that he could. Cornelius, the godly centurion, who was the first-fruits of the Gentiles, had not been bidden to give up his profession. One of the younger men, whose temper was fiery, almost fanatical, took the opposite view. The soldier was essentially a man of the world, and the world was at enmity with the Church. Nor could Fabius hide from himself the difficulties. Idolatry was everywhere. His arms, for instance, bore the images of gods; to be present at sacrifice to gods was a frequent duty; worst of all, he would himself be called upon to sacrifice by burning incense before the image of the Emperor. All this had made him hesitate.

"Do you know their place of meeting?" asked the Governor.

Fabius assented.

"And the time?"

To answer readily would have been to betray too intimate a knowledge of the Christians' proceedings.

"Doubtless," my lord," he said, despising himself at the same time for the prevarication, "I can find it out."

"Then take a guard on the first occasion that occurs, and arrest in the name of the Emperor all that you may find assembled."

"It shall be done, my lord," said Fabius, still unmoved, and, after saluting, withdrew.

No one would have recognized the centurion Fabius, with his almost mechanical rigidity of movement, in the agitated man who, for the next hour, paced up and down in his chamber. It is to be feared that he wished over and over again that this disturbing influence had never come into his life. Here was a conflict of duties such as he had never even dreamed of. Could he let these men and women whom he knew, some of whom had been so kind to him, who would have done all they could for him, run blindly into danger? And yet, would it not be a breach of duty to warn them? The Governor trusted him; the charge laid upon him was a secret. Could he, as a soldier, betray it? Again and again he made up his mind, only to unmake it the next moment. At last the struggle ended, as such struggles often do, in a compromise; and here circumstances helped him. The meeting would be the next day, he knew; and it was now afternoon. There would not be time to warn all the members of the community, even had he known—what he did not know—where they were to be found. But there was one to whom word must be sent at any cost. This was Rhoda, the daughter of Bion. Fabius had been one of the many who had been struck by the girl's singular beauty. Like his rivals, he had seen that her heart had no room for any earthly love. Still, he cherished her image as one might cherish the vision of an angel. To think of her in the rude hands of soldiers, or dragged to the common prison, was simply intolerable. That must be prevented, if it cost him his officer's rank, or even his honour.

No sooner had he made up his mind to send the girl a warning message, than, as if by the ordering of some higher Power, an opportunity presented itself to him. He caught sight of one of Bion's slaves, who was driving down the street an ass laden with farm produce. To accost the man as he passed might have raised suspicion. A safer plan would be to waylay him as he returned, which he would scarcely do before evening was drawing on. And this he was able to carry out without, as he felt sure, being observed by any one. He thrust into the hands of the old man—a faithful creature, whom he knew to be deeply attached to Bion and his family—a letter thus inscribed:—

"Fabius the Centurion, to Rhoda, daughter of Bion.

"I implore you that to-morrow you remain at home. This shall be well both for you and for those whom you love. Farewell."

7

THE ARREST

THE centurion's message was duly delivered to Rhoda, nor, thought it failed in its immediate object, was it sent wholly in vain. The girl herself never for one moment entertained the idea of profiting by the warning so as to secure her own safety. She would have been even capable of suppressing it altogether, if she could have been quite as sure of others as she was of herself. There was nothing that she felt to be more desirable that the martyr's crown, and why should she hinder those who were dear to her from attaining the same glory? But these high-wrought feelings had not wholly banished common sense. She was perfectly well aware that such aspirations were beyond the average capacity of her fellow-creatures. She doubted whether her own sister was equal to them. She was quite sure that some of her fellow-believers would fail under the fiery trial of martyrdom, and she shrank from the peril of exposing them to it. Nothing could be more dreadful than that they should fall away and deny their Lord. It would be a deadly sin in them, and, to say the least, a lifelong remorse to her, if she should have led them into such temptation. Her mind was soon made up. Her first step was to find her father, and give him the warning, only keeping back, as she felt bound to do, the name of her informant. Bion, whose practical good sense told him that dangers come quickly enough without one's going to meet them, resolved to keep all his family at home. Under ordinary circumstances, knowing the temper of his elder daughter, he would have charged her on his obedience not to venture out. But Rhoda's action in freely coming to him with the warning that she had received, put him off his guard. He took it for granted that she would attend to it herself, and, not a little to her relief, let her go without exacting any promise from her.

The next morning she started earlier than usual for the place of meeting. Her hope was to see the Elders, communicate what she knew to them, and leave the matter in their hands. They would know what was best for their people. If they judged it better that the disciples should hide from the storm rather than meet it, she would obey their decision, whatever might be her own disappointment. If, as she hoped, their counsel should be "to resist unto blood," then she would be there to share the glorious peril.

One of the little accidents, as we call them, that so often come in to hinder the carrying out of great plans, hindered Rhoda from accomplishing her design. She started at an earlier hour than usual, before there was even a glimmer of twilight, and instead of being more careful than was her want in picking her way along the rough lane that led from the farmhouse into the public road, was, in her haste, more heedless. Before she had gone fifty yards from the house, she stumbled on a stone, and for some moments felt as if she could not move another step. Then her resolute spirit came to her help. "To think of the martyr's crown, and then be daunted by a sprained ankle!" she said to herself; and she struggled on. But all the courage in the world could not give her back her usual speed of foot; so that the hour of meeting had already passed while she was still some distance from the chapel. She was still crawling along when another of the worshippers, a young slave who had been detained at home by some work which he could not finish in time, overtook her. She at once made up her mind that he must act as her messenger, and that the message must be as brief and emphatic as possible.

The young man halted when he recognised her figure, saluted her, and asked whether he could give her any help.

"Leave me, Dromio", she answered, "leave me to shift for myself; but run with all the speed you can tell the Elder Anicetus that there is danger."

Dromio waited for no second bidding. He started off at once at the top of his speed, and as he was vigorous and fleet of foot, he reached the place of assembly in a very few minutes.

The celebration of the Holy Communion was going on, and the congregation was engaged in silent prayer previous to the distribution of the bread and wine, when the breathless messenger, pushing aside the door-keeper who would have barred his entrance at what seemed so inopportune a time, burst into the midst.

"Venerable Anicetus," cried the young man, "there is danger!"

Such alarms were not unknown in those perilous times, and though the congregation was startled, there was nothing like panic.

Anicetus, a veteran in the service of his Master, and a confessor who had stood more than once in peril of his life, kept all his presence of mind.

"Be calm, my son," he said; "tell me whence or from whom you bring this message."

"I bring it from Rhoda the deaconess"—for as such the girl was known, though, as has been said before, she had not been formally admitted to the order—"I overtook her on my way hither. She was limping along, in pain as it seemed, though she said nothing, and she bade me hasten on, and deliver this message."

"It is no false alarm," said the elder, "if it came from our sister Rhoda. Saw you or heard you any signs of an enemy as you came?"

"I saw and heard nothing," answered Dromio.

"And you came from the town?"

"Yes, from the town."

"Then the soldiers have not yet started," said the old man in an undertone to himself, "and we have a few moments to think."

By common consent the whole assembly waited for his decision. This deference was not so much paid to his office as to the man. Ordinarily such a matter would have been discussed by the community. But Anicetus was one of the men to whom in a time of peril all look for guidance. After a very brief pause for deliberation he spoke.

"All brethren and sisters that are of the servile condition will depart at once, and do their best to escape the soldiers."

There were doubtless one or two bolder spirits among the male slaves who murmured inwardly at this command. But they obeyed it without hesitation. Indeed, they knew only too well the cogent force or the reasoning which dictated it. A free man or woman was exempted by law from torture, but it might be applied to a slave; and it would be applied almost certainly to some at least of those who might be arrested in the act of attending an unlawful assembly. If, on the other hand, they could escape for the time, their masters, even for the mere selfish motive of saving valuable property damage, would do their best to protect them. It was well, therefore, to get them out of the way, both for their own sake and for the sake of the community. The Church had found many times what a horribly effective instrument her persecutors had in this power of torturing the slaves. It was not that she dreaded the truth that they might be thus compelled to speak, it was the falsehoods that might be forced out of them that were so much to be feared. Again and again, miserable creatures, whose courage had broken down under this pitiless infliction, had purchased relief from their sufferings by inventing hideous charges against their brethren. The mere truth had not satisfied the persecutor, who often really believed that there must be something more behind; and so they had been driven, as it were, to lie.

When the slaves were gone, Anicetus spoke again: "Brethren and sisters, you must be brave; that, I do not doubt, you will be. And you must be prudent; that, to some of you, will be less easy. Therefore I warn you. Court no danger. You shall have strength for your day, but not beyond it. When you are accused, be silent—as far as you may. The law does not compel you to bring peril upon yourselves, and they cannot force you to speak. Acts unlawful to a Christian you will, of course, refuse. There you will not yield so much as a hair's breadth. But see that these acts be such as may lawfully be demanded of you.

This is the counsel that I give you, so far as things of this life are concerned. Spiritual help you will not lack, if, indeed, you have not believed in vain. And now, while there is yet time, let us strengthen ourselves with the Communion of the Body and Blood of our Lord. It shall be provision for a way that may lie through rough places."

Just as the Elder had finished speaking, Rhoda entered the chapel. The strength that had supported her through her painful journey failed when she reached its end, and she sank, almost fainting, on the floor. Two of the women helped her into a little antechamber, and gave her such comfort and relief as was possible. Meanwhile the interrupted rite went on. The little congregation again offered up their hearts in silent prayer—not less earnest, we may be sure, than that which had been broken into by the arrival of the messenger of danger. This ended, the sacred Bread and Wine were administered: with what depth of feeling in ministers and people it is impossible for us to realize, whether (as will be the case with most who read these lines) we are living quiet and peaceful lives, or even are brought face to face with great perils, such as the perils of the sea and the battle-field. To "resist unto blood," as these weak men and women were called to do, wanted an enthusiasm of courage far greater than is needed for the lifeboat or the forlorn hope.

The Communion was almost ended when a loud knocking on the door of the meeting-house showed that the soldiers had come. The Centurion Fabius had not ventured to evade the duty of executing in person the order of the Governor; but to make the actual arrest was more than he could bring himself to endure. To enter the chapel on such an errand would have been an intolerable profanation. Happily, military etiquette permitted him to delegate this duty to his deputy. It was this officer, who had been duly cautioned to perform his office as gently as he could, who now presented himself at the chapel door. It was thrown open at once. One point that the Christians were always careful to insist upon was that, though they might find it prudent to meet in secret, they had nothing to conceal. Anicetus was just about to administer the Bread and Wine to Rhoda—who was now partially recovered—when the deputy centurion entered the building. With a gesture of command, which the rough soldier felt himself strangely constrained to obey, he motioned the man back, and then, without a change of look or voice, performed his sacred office.

The rite finished, he turned to the soldier, and courteously asked him his errand. The man produced the Governor's order to arrest all the persons who should be found assembled in the guild-house of the wool-combers. Anicetus perused the document deliberately, and then returned it to the officer, with the words, "It seems to be in order. We are ready to obey."

The number of prisoners who had been thus taken was a few less than forty, of whom six, including Rhoda, were women. The men were lightly bound—that is, the right arm of one was attached to the left arm of another. The old knight Antistius, and the Elder Anicetus, both of whom were Roman citizens, were not subjected to this indignity; nor was it thought necessary to secure the women.

The question then arose, What was to be done with Rhoda, who was clearly unable to walk? The deputy consulted his chief.

"There is a woman among the arrested," he said, "whom it will be necessary to carry, if she is to accompany the others. Will you be pleased to give your commands?"

No sooner had Fabius heard these words than an agonizing suspicion of the truth crossed his mind. Something, he knew not what, told him that this disabled woman could be no other than Rhoda herself. The wild idea of making this a pretext for releasing her occurred to him, only to be dismissed the next moment. She could not be left; and if she was to be taken, she must go with the rest. With a sinking heart he entered the chapel, and a single glance at her figure, though her face was turned from him, convinced him that his fears had not been vain. It was Rhoda. His warning had been fruitless, although a hasty glance showed him that neither Bion nor Cleoné was among the prisoners. She had been more careful for others than for herself.

It was agony to Fabius to feel that he was the man to put her into the hands of her enemies, and he was glad to leave the chapel before she could recognize him.

Meanwhile the practical difficulty had been solved by an ingenious soldier who had fetched a bier from the mortuary of the burial ground. A little contrivance converted this into a litter. It was convenient enough, and was made comfortable with the cloaks of the party; but Fabius shuddered at the sight of the living borne on the vehicle of the dead.

The departure of the soldiers from the town had not been unnoticed, and a crowd was assembled to witness their return. The principal street was indeed thronged with the spectators as the prisoners were marched along it to the Governor's quarters. A few groans and hisses were heard at one point, where Arruns with some of his friends had stationed himself; but on the whole the feeling was friendly rather than hostile. Few knew much about these Christians, but men had already begun to find out that they were friends of the sick, the poor, the unhappy.

8

BEFORE THE GOVERNOR

THE arrest at the chapel had been made so early that it still wanted more than an hour of noon when the prisoners were brought into the presence of the Governor. Pliny, aware of the importance of the case which he was about to try, had called in the help of a trained lawyer—an advocate of high reputation—who had some time before retired from his profession, and who now sat as his assessor. At the same time he had invited Tacitus, as a senator and ex-consul, to take a seat on the bench. The prosecution was conducted by the principal lawyer of the town, and Lucilius, Arruns, with several of the Nicæan merchants, supported him by their presence. The accused, numbering more than thirty in all, of whom two thirds belonged to the labouring class, were undefended. All the slaves had contrived to escape arrest. The lower part of the hall was densely crowded with a mass of interested spectators. All available space, indeed, had been filled up within a few minutes of the arrival of the prisoners, and the approaches to the hall were thronged by eager candidates for admission.

When the prisoners had answered to their names, and had stated their several occupations and condition of life, the inquiry began. A long harangue by the prosecutor on the subject of the importance of the worship of the gods was cut short by the Governor, who intimated that his eloquence, if it should be wanted at all, would be more relevant after his evidence had been produced. Thus checked, the advocate began his examination, addressing it in the first instance to Anicetus.

"You are one of the leaders of the society which calls itself by the name of Christus?'

"Is this the matter, or among the matters, of which you accuse me?"

"Certainly it is."

"Then you hold it to be a crime to belong to this society of Christus?"

"Certainly, seeing that it is not one of the societies that are permitted to exist by the constitution of the Roman Sate and the will of our sovereign lord, Trajan Augustus."

"If that be so, I appeal to the Governor whether by the law of Rome I can be compelled to make such answer as would criminate myself."

The appeal was so manifestly just that the Governor did not think it necessary to consult his assessor, but decided that the question need not be answered.

Baffled at this point, the prosecutor re-commenced his attack at another.

"You do not deny that you and your associates were assembled this morning in the guild-house of the wool-combers?"

"We do not deny it."

"For what purpose, then, did you meet?"

"Before I answer that question, I would myself wish to know whether you have the right to ask it. Are free men and women, against whom there is no evidence of wrong-doing, to be questioned by any one as to the purpose of their meeting? That we have the right to use the guild-house of the wool-combers is proved by this document."

So saying, Anicetus produced from his pocket a small parchment, which simply recited that the wool-combers, in consideration of a sum of four hundred drachmæ yearly, permitted the use of their guild-house to Anicetus.

"You see, then," resumed Anicetus, "that we have not taken possession of a place to which we are not entitled, nor is there any evidence against us of unlawful dealings. Were we found with weapons in our hands, or preparing noxious drugs, or practising forbidden acts, or plotting against the safety of the State and the life of the Emperor, then might you justly ask us for our defence. But you do not attempt to prove against us any unlawful deed or words."

The prosecutor then tried a third method of attack. "Are you and your associates willing to worship the gods of the Roman State, and to pay the customary homage to the image of our lord, Trajan Augustus?"

Without answering this question Anicetus turned to the governor: "Is it permitted to us, most excellent Plinius, that we see the accusation under which we have been this day brought before you?"

"There are many accusations," replied the Governor; "they are substantially the same, and it will probably suffice for the purpose that one should be read.—Scribe," he went on, turning to an official that sat near, "read the information of Lucilius against the people called Christians."

The document was read. It charged a number of persons, including all of the prisoners then before the court, and many who were not in custody. Treason, impiety towards the gods and towards the Emperor, hatred of mankind, licentiousness, were among the accusations brought against them.

"Here," said Anicetus, when the reading was finished, "are many terrible things brought against us, whereof no proof has been given by our accuser. Is it lawful, most excellent Plinius, that, such proof failing him, he should seek thus to raise prejudice against us? What right has this advocate, being but a private person, to call upon his fellow-citizens to do sacrifice to the gods or to the Emperor? What right has he to fix the time, the place, the manner of worship? Were an Egyptian, a worshipper of Isis, standing here, could he be lawfully compelled to do sacrifice to Jupiter? Or should a German—a worshipper, as I have heard, of Hertha—be condemned because he does not pay reverence to Apollo? For tell me now," he went on, addressing the accuser, "you that charge us with impiety, are you diligent in the performance of your own duties in divine things?"

The accuser was notoriously a man who believed in nothing, and was known not to spend a drachma on any religious duty. A hum of approval ran round the court at this manifest hit. So far, the line of defence taken by Anicetus had been successful. It might easily have failed with another Governor, a man of more imperious and tyrannical temper than Pliny; but the Elder had skillfully taken into account the Governor's mild and tolerant character, and his probable desire to avoid any measure of severity. But it was now to be overthrown in an unexpected way. A tablet was passed from among the crowd of spectators and put into the hands of the prosecuting counsel. On it were written the words, "Challenge the free condition of Rhoda, commonly called the daughter of Bion and Rhoda his wife, and call as your witness the freedman Eudoxus." This document bore the name of Lucilius, and the prosecutor at once perceived its importance. Indeed, it was his last hope, if his case was not to break down completely. He resumed his address.

"As your regard for freedom, most excellent Plinius, protects the silence of Anicetus and his companions, I will address myself to the case of one of the accused who cannot claim this same protection. I maintain that the woman Rhoda—the reputed daughter of Bion and Rhoda—is not of free condition, but is a slave."

Had a thunderbolt fallen in the court, judge, assessor, accused, and audience could not have been more astonished. The first feeling was one of absolute incredulity. To no one did the statement seem more absurd than to the girl herself.

"This is a strange contention," remarked the Governor, "and not lightly to be made against a family of good repute. What evidence can you produce?"

"I call the freedman Eudoxus," replied the prosecutor.

The freedman Eudoxus was present, it soon appeared, in court, for he answered when his name was called. Most of those present knew him, but none, it may safely be said, knew any good of him. He did a little pettifogging business as an informer—a person who performs functions that may sometimes be useful, but are certainly always odious. If a baker gave short weight, if a wine-seller hammered the sides or thickened the bottoms of his measures, Eudoxus was commonly the man to bring his misdeeds home to him, getting for his reward half the penalty. Had he been content with this, he might have been endured; but he was not content—his gains had to be increased. If he did not find offences he manufactured them. All the little traders and shopkeepers of the place—for he did not fly at high game—were in terror of him, and most of them submitted to the blackmail which he levied of them. As he spent his ill-gotten gains in the most discreditable way, it may be guessed that Eudoxus had about as bad a reputation as any one in Nicæa. Great was the wonder among the audience what this miserable creature could know about the family of the respectable Bion. A few of the older people, however, had the impression that he had once been in the farmer's employment.

Eudoxus, a man of dwarfish stature, with a large misshapen head, whose countenance bore manifest tokens of a life of excess, stood up in the witness- box. The usual oath was administered to him.

"Tell us," said the Governor, "what you know about this case."

"Twenty years ago I was in the service of Bion. He is my patron. He enfranchised me. I was his bailiff."

"Why did you leave him?" asked the Governor.

"We had a difference about my accounts."

"I understand," said Pliny, who, like the rest of the world, was not impressed with the appearance of the witness; "you made things better for yourself and worse for him than he thought right. But go on; what do you know about this matter? You understand what it is; practically this, that the accused Rhoda is not truly the daughter of Bion. Do you know this said Rhoda?"

"Perfectly well, and her sister Cleoné also."

"Proceed then."

"Bion bought me about a month after he came to the farm which he now cultivates. I was there when he brought thither his newly married wife, Rhoda by name. I lived in the house for five years following that time. They had no children. Of this I am sure, for I saw the said Rhoda day after day, without the intermission of more than a day at the most, during the said five years. It was a matter of common talk among us of the household that this want of children was a great grief to the master and his wife. There years after his coming, one morning—it was, I remember, the first day of May—Bion called us all into the dining-chamber. There was a cradle with two children in it. I should judge that they were a few days old. He said, 'See the daughters whom God has given me.' The same day he enfranchised me. To the other slaves he gave presents, and promised them their liberty in due time, according to their age, if they should show themselves worthy of it."

"He called them his daughters, then?" asked the Governor.

"Truly; but no pretence was made that they were so in truth, for his wife did not keep her chamber."

"Who were the women that waited upon her? Are they yet alive?"

"The elder, who was called the mistress's nurse, died, I believe, some ten years since. The younger is married to Lucas the butcher, that has his stall in the north-east corner of the market-place."

The Governor gave directions that the wife of Lucas the butcher should be sent for. Meanwhile he adjourned the proceedings for half an hour.

On the re-assembling of the court the witness was ready to be examined. Happily for herself, as will be seen, she had been emancipated before her marriage. She gave her testimony with evident reluctance, but it was clear and conclusive.

"I was waiting-maid of Rhoda, wife of Bion. Bion bought me of a dealer in Ephesus a few days before his marriage, that I might wait on his wife. I went to her at once, and never left her till I was married, now ten years ago. She never had a child born to her. It is impossible that she should have done so without my knowing. It was commonly said that this was a great grief to her. I have seen her weeping, and knew that this was the cause. One day, when I had been with her about three years, the old woman whom we used commonly to call her nurse said to me: 'Come now, Myrto'—that was my name—'see the mistress's lovely babies.'—'What?' I said; 'it is impossible.'—'Nay, say nothing,' she said, and put her hand on my mouth. Then she took me into a chamber next to the mistress's, and sure enough, there were two lovely little girl-babies, twins, as one could see at once, not more than a few days old, as I judged. Nurse said, 'You are a wise girl, and can keep a quiet tongue in your head. From to-day these two are Rhoda and Cleoné, daughters of Bion and Rhoda. And now, mind, not a word to any one; and, above all, not a word to the little ones themselves when they grow up. For love's sake, I know, you will keep silence, nor will you miss your reward.'"

"And did you know whose the children really were?" asked the Governor.

"I did not know."

"Could they have belonged to any one in the household?"

"Certainly not. Of this I am sure."

"Some one, I suppose, knew?"

"Yes, nurse knew, but she never told. She has been dead some years. The matter was never mentioned. We were the only women in the house. Eudoxus was the only man. The other slaves were outdoor laborers. None of them, as far as I know, are in this neighbourhood now. The girls, when they grew up, always supposed that they were the daughters of the house. It was never doubted; nothing was ever said to make a doubt."

The witness, whose self-control utterly broke down as soon as she had finished her evidence, now left the box. After a brief consultation with his assessor and with Tacitus, the Governor directed that Bion and Rhoda his wife should be called.

The two were of course present. One of the slaves who had left the assembly, at the bidding of Anicetus, had made them acquainted with Rhoda's proceedings. As the girl herself failed to return at the usual time, their fears were aroused, and they were turned into certainty by the news that reached them from the town that a large company of Christians had been arrested at their meeting-house. On hearing these tidings they had hurried down to the town, accompanied by Cleoné, whom nothing indeed could at such a time have kept away from her sister.

The two answered to their names.

"Let Rhoda, the reputed mother of the person whose condition is questioned, be first called," said the Governor.

A way was made for her through the throng with no little difficulty, and she made her way with tottering steps and face pale as death, into the witness-box.

"You have heard," said the Governor, "the testimony of Eudoxus, and Myrto the wife of Lucas?"

"I have heard," she answered.

"Nevertheless, for the more assurance, let the depositions be read over."

A scribe accordingly read the depositions.

'What have you to say to this evidence?"

The unhappy woman did not hesitate a moment. Nothing could have induced her to go aside by one hair's-breadth from the truth. She lifted her eyes, looked the Governor in the face and answered in a low firm voice: "It is true. The children are not mine."

"And do you know whose children they are?"

"I know not."

"Nor whence they came?"

"Not even that. My nurse, as I called her, said that I had best not know. I think that they had been deserted; but even of this I am not sure. I can only guess it, because I never heard so much as a word about the parents. Nurse would never speak on the subject. Even when she was dying—for I was with her, and asked her again, as I thought it right to do—she would tell me nothing. 'They are your children by the will of God,' she said; 'no one else has part or lot in them.'"

A whispered consultation now took place between the Governor and his assessor. As the result of it, Bion was called.

"You have heard," said the Governor, "the testimony of your wife. What say you to it?"

It would have been useless to deny it, even if Bion, who was as truthful as his wife, could have wished to do so. "It is true," he said.

"Do you know whence the children came?"

"I know nothing more than my wife. The nurse knew, but she would say no more to me than she would to her."

"Then you cannot say whether they are bond or free by birth?"

The force of the question did not strike the witness, overpowered as he was by the situation, though there were many in the court who saw its significance, while an evil smile crept over the face of the prosecutor.

"Free, my lord!" he answered, after a pause; "of course they are free—they are my adopted children."

The Governor saw the course that things were taking, and was glad to leave the matter to the prosecutor, being ready to interfere if he saw a chance of helping the imperilled women.

"Excuse me, sir," said the prosecutor; "you speak of them as being your adopted children, but can you produce the instrument of adoption?"

The poor man was staggered by the question. "I never adopted them in that way. I never thought it necessary. But I have treated them as my children; they have lived with us as children. I have divided everything that I have between them in my will."

"Pardon me," said the prosecutor, with his voice most studiously gentle, and his smile more falsely sweet, as he saw his toils closing round his prey, "I do not doubt your kindness to them; but if you cannot produce the usual legal instrument—which, indeed, I understand you to say you have never executed—they are not your adopted children. And if you have not adopted them, may I ask whether you have emancipated them?"

The purport of the examination now made itself clear to the unhappy man. He had, of course, done nothing of the kind. Taking it for granted that their condition would never be questioned—ignorant, too, of law, as a man of his training and occupation would almost certainly be—he had never dreamt of either adopting or emancipating the two girls. He had simply treated them as his daughters, and never doubted for a moment that all the world would do so likewise.

"I have established then, most excellent sir," said the prosecutor, "that the woman Rhoda and her sister Cleoné, with whom, indeed, I am not at present concerned, are of the condition of slaves. I demand, therefore, that the woman Rhoda be questioned in the customary way."

The Governor interposed, "Doubtless the accused will answer such questions as will be put to her."

"Pardon me, sir, if I say that the law knows but one way only of questioning a slave."

"But if the slave be willing to speak?"

"Even then, I submit, the law presumes that he will speak the truth only under this compulsion. I demand, therefore, that the woman Rhoda be questioned by torture."

A movement of horror went through the whole assembly.

Another consultation followed between the Governor and his assessor. "This seems to me a needless severity," said Pliny, when it was finished. "Why not reserve this compulsion if the witness should be obstinate?"

The prosecuting counsel, hardened as he was, was staggered by this appeal. He turned to Lucilius for further instructions. Lucilius was pitiless. He had been enraged by the cool and skilful defence of Anicetus, and he was determined not to lose his grasp on the victim that had fallen into his power. "Keep to your point," he whispered to the accuser.

"I demand the question by torture against the woman Rhoda."

"It is granted," said the Governor, "but so that nothing that she shall say be used against Bion and Rhoda his wife."

Cleoné, who was standing by the side of the elder Rhoda, had gone on hoping against hope till the fatal words were spoken. Then she rushed forward and caught her sister in her arms. "We will suffer together," she said.

9

RHODA'S EVIDENCE

THE Elder felt that his position, so to speak, had been turned. His silence, however skilfully justified, was useless —nay, it was worse than useless, for it had brought this daughter of the Church, one for whom they would all gladly have suffered, into terrible peril. They had escaped for the time; but at what a cost, if Rhoda was to be tortured!

He made a last effort to save her. "My lord," he said, "I withdraw my refusal to speak. Any questions that you or the prosecutor may put to me I will answer; and what I say for myself, I say also for all the accused."

"What say you to this?" asked the Governor.

There was another brief consultation between the advocate and Lucilius. Then the former rose.

"My lord, our interest, our only interest, is the truth. Our aim, and, I presume, the aim of all persons not being criminal or hostile to the State, is that the truth should be fully told, and amply confirmed. Therefore we must have the best evidence that can be procured, nor can we allow our private feelings to hinder its forthcoming. Is it not a maxim of the law that when slaves are at hand you do not use the testimony of freemen, it being agreed that the truth is more surely drawn forth by the more powerful compulsion?"

The Governor referred the point to his assessor, and that official decided, though with evident reluctance, that the contention was just.

Nothing now stood between the prisoner and her fate. The instrument of torture was sent for. Whilst it was being brought there was a terrible pause of expectation in the court. Tacitus rose as if to leave the room, but a whispered entreaty from the Governor made him resume his seat. In the audience the agitation was extreme. Several persons fainted; many, both men and women, burst into uncontrollable weeping. The least troubled of all was the girl herself. There was something more than calm on her countenance; there was exaltation—almost, it might be said, rapture. Even as it had been with the judges of Stephen—for so we learn from the confession of one of their number—those who looked upon her saw her face "as it had been the face of an angel."

The instrument of torture was something like a rack. The savage humour which gives a half-comic name to these hideous implements of cruelty had invented for it the nickname of the "Little Horse." The resemblance lay in the four beams, projecting from a timber frame, to which the limbs of the sufferer were attached.

Before this was done the Governor ordered the court to be cleared of all persons not immediately interested in the trial. A few heartless creatures were probably disappointed that their curiosity was not to be gratified; but most of the spectators, however intense their interest, felt the order to be a relief. Bion and his wife claimed to be allowed to remain. It would break their hearts to see such a sight, but their presence might comfort the sufferer; and as she was their slave, if not their daughter, their claim was, of course, allowed. The elder Rhoda's whole thought was centred on the desire to minister to this, the child of her heart if not the child of her womb. Bion watched what was done with a set, tearless face, crushing down the wild impulse to fly to the sufferer's rescue. Most of the spectators averted their eyes; even Lucilius was seen to bury his face in a fold of his toga.

The preparations were now complete, and the executioner awaited the signal of the judge to commence his hideous task. This was given by a gesture, and the man immediately followed it up by the first turn of the dreadful instrument. No one who was present that day ever forgot the horrible creaking sound of the timbers, mingled with a groan of the sufferer, forced from her by the pain, but stifled almost as soon as uttered. There was not a heart, not even of the ruthless Lucilius, in which the blood did not curdle; not a forehead on which the cold drops of sweat did not stand.

The Governor thundered, in a voice such as had never been heard to issue from his lips before: "Hold!"

The executioner, brutalized as he was by familiarity with the horrid details of his office, was not sorry to stay his hand.

The Governor went on: "The law has so far been satisfied. The torture has been applied, and in my judgment, which in this matter is final, has been applied sufficiently. If the accused is now willing to make confession, I will hear her."

Rhoda was unfastened from the rack. The executioner assisted her to rise; but she could not stand, and the Governor directed that a seat should be provided for her. "Now," he said to the prosecutor, "put your questions."

"Are you one of the people that are called Christians?"

"I am."

"Are you accustomed to assemble together?"

"We are so accustomed."

"On what days, and at what time?"

"Once in seven days at the least, and at other times also. The hour of our assembling is before daybreak."

"And what do you at these gatherings?"

"We offer up prayers, and sing praises to God."

"To what god?"

"To God Almighty, who made the heavens and the earth, and is the Father of all men."

"Who, then, is this Christus by whose name you are called?"

"He is God."

"Then you worship two gods—the Father, of whom you speak, and Christus?"

"Nay, for Christus is the Son of the Father, and they two are one God. But ask me not to explain these matters, for I am unlearned in them."

"Is there anything else that you do when you have finished these prayers and hymns?"

"These being finished we depart to our own homes. But in the evening of the same day we meet together and have our Feast of Love."

"With what preparations do you make this feast? With what dainties in meat and drink is it furnished?"

"The preparation is of the very simplest; there is nothing, indeed, beyond bread and wine."

"Why do you take such trouble to do that which is easier done in your own homes?"

"Because it has been so commanded us by our Master, that we may remember Him and His death for us, and may also show forth the love by which we are bound one to another."

"Do you, then, all sit down together at this feast?"

"Yes, we all sit down; nor is there any distinction made of rich and poor, bond and free."

"And do you bind yourselves by any oath?"

"Yes, if you will have it so, for this very feast is an oath to us."

"And to what does this oath constrain you?"

"That we should neither kill, nor steal, nor commit uncleanness, nor break a promise, nor refuse when called upon to account for moneys committed to our charge."

"Does this oath concern at all the Emperor and the State?"

"Only so far that we are bound to be loyal and obedient."

"Obedient in all things?"

"In all things that are lawful to us as followers of the Lord Christ."

"I pray you, my lord, to take a note of this reservation," said the prosecutor, addressing this observation to the Governor. He then proceeded with his examination of the prisoner. "Can you tell the names of others who were accustomed to be present at these assemblies?"

The girl hesitated for a moment when this question was put to her. Then she spoke with a firm voice: "Concerning myself I will speak the truth, nor seek to conceal anything; but of others I am not free to speak."

The Elder did not lose a moment in intervening at this point. "Permit me, my lord," he said addressing the Governor, "to admit for myself, and for all that are here present with me that we are of the people called Christians."

The prosecutor proceeded with his examination of Rhoda. "Can you tell us the names of others not here present?"

"Nay," interrupted the Governor; "on behalf of the absent, whom the magistrate is always especially bound to protect, I disallow that question."

The prosecutor then turned to the Elder: "Are you a ruler among these people?"

"Yes, if you will have it so. I am, as it were, the first among the brethren; but if they obey me it is of their own free will."

"Yet they are accustomed to follow your advice?"

"Certainly; they are so accustomed."

"Do you know that his Excellency the Governor, by command of our lord Trajan, issued an edict by which it was forbidden to hold unlawful assemblies?"

"Yes, I knew that such an edict was issued."

"Did you, therefore, cease to hold your assemblies?—though, indeed, seeing that you are year to-day, I need scarcely ask this question."

"We did not cease to hold them."

"Was the matter debated among you?"

This was a difficult question to answer. The matter had been debated, and that with considerable energy, in the Christian community. Some, of a more timorous spirit, had advised that the assemblies should cease; but Anicetus had been firm for their continuance. It would be a risk to hold them, for it might bring the Church into conflict with the law; but the spiritual danger, the dangers of growing coldness, of want of faith, of laxity of practice, that would follow on their discontinuance, were, in his view, much more serious. Prudent Christian that he was, and anxious to avoid a conflict of which he could not see the end, his voice had been given without hesitation for disregarding the edict, or, at least, treating it as if it did not apply. A division had followed. Some members of the community had preferred to follow the safer course. The majority had held with Anicetus, and the assemblies had gone on without interruption. Nothing, of course, remained for him now but to speak the truth.

"It was debated. We differed in opinion. I held that the edict did not apply to us, and advised my brethren accordingly. Some thought differently, and came no more to our meetings."

This frank reply gave a very serious appearance to the whole affair. It could hardly be otherwise regarded than as an avowal of guilt, or at least of what was guilt in the eye of Roman law. The Governor, who had begun the inquiry with a feeling of tolerance, and had become more and more favourably disposed to the accused as it proceeded, was adversely impressed by it. He seemed to see himself face to face with the invincible obstinacy of which he had been warned. Still, he would gladly have sheltered the accused if he could. His own private opinion was that the Emperor's opposition to what were called secret societies was over-strained and excessive. No trace of loose behaviour or mischievous aims could be found in these people. He was unwilling to condemn, and yet, in view of their own admission, he could not acquit them. The only thing that remained was to postpone the trial. If a time for consideration were given, perhaps some compromise might become possible. This accordingly was the course on which he determined.

"I postpone this inquiry," he announced, "till the ides of May [the 15th]. The prisoners will be released on giving bail. The woman Rhoda will be delivered to her master Bion, who will give sufficient surety for producing her when she shall be required."

The court was then adjourned.

10

THE EXAMINATION

THE Governor's advisers did their best to deepen the adverse impression made upon his mind by the frank admission of the Elder. The philosophical Tacitus was especially urgent in his advice that this "execrable superstition," as he called it, should be rooted out. With others of the more thoughtful Roman statesmen, he saw quite plainly that this new faith was really the enemy of the old system of the Empire, and would destroy it if it were not itself destroyed. It was generally the best Emperors who were the persecutors of the Church. A weak tyrant might happen to indulge in some outbreak of caprice or cruelty; but the steady, systematic hostility—the hostility that was really dangerous—came from vigorous rulers: from such men as Aurelius, and Decius, and Diocletian. Tacitus accordingly was, even vehemently, on the side of severity; and Pliny, who always leaned on the stronger character of his friend, resolved to follow his advice.

Something like a reign of terror followed in Nicæa and the neighbourhood. A regular inquisition was made of all who were known or suspected to be Christians. The informers (who, as we know, had already been at work) became more busy than ever. Long lists of accused persons were drawn up, and, as usual at such times, private spite and malice found their opportunity. A jealous lover put down the name of a rival on the list, and a debtor thought it a good way of ridding himself of a troublesome creditor. As lists were received even without being signed, or with signatures about which no inquiry was made, scarcely any one could consider himself safe.

It was a formidable array of prisoners that was gathered on the day of the adjourned trial in the public hall of Nicæa, no room in the Governor's palace being sufficiently large to receive them. On this occasion all spectators were excluded, and the approaches to the hall were strongly guarded with troops. Within, the arrangements for the trial were much the same as before, except that an officer of the local military force sat below the bench occupied by the Governor and his assessors, in charge of a bust of the Emperor; and that a small movable altar had been arranged in front, with a brazier full of lighted coals upon it.

Anicetus and his companions, who had been arraigned on the occasion already described, were first called to answer to their names. Their cases would, it was thought, take but little time, for they had already confessed to the fact of being Christians. The only question was, Would they adhere to that confession or retract it?

We sometimes think that all the Christians of those early times, when the profession of the faith was never a mere matter of inheritance or fashion, were true to their Master in the face of all dangers, and under the pressure of the worst tortures. But this is a delusion. Human nature was weak then, as now. Men fell away under temptation, either because they had not a firm enough grasp of the truth which they professed, or because there was some weakness—it may be, some cherished sin—in them that sapped their strength. Sometimes, one can hardly doubt, God, for his own good purposes, suffered even His faithful servants to fall away from Him for a time. St. Paul hints as much when, describing his career as a persecutor in his defence before Festus and Agrippa, he says "he compelled" the objects of his hatred "to blaspheme." And we know that some of the bitterest and fiercest controversies of the early Church concerned the treatment of the lapsi, as they were called—those who had fallen away from their profession. One would gladly draw a veil over the weakness of these unhappy creatures, but to do so would make the picture of the time less faithful.

The first prisoner called upon for his answer by the Governor was the Elder. He, at all events, did not show the faintest sign of yielding.

The Governor addressed him: "You declared when you were last brought before me that you were a Christian. Do you still abide by that declaration?"

"I do," said the old man, in an unfaltering voice.

"Are you willing to burn incense to the likeness of our sovereign lord Trajan?"

"I am not willing."

"Not when I impose upon you the duty of thus proving that you are a loyal citizen?"

"Loyal I am, nor can any man prove that I have erred in this respect; but this I refuse."

"You refuse, then, to obey the commands of the Emperor himself? Listen."

The Governor produced a parchment, from which, after kissing it, he read these words: "I enjoin on my lieutenants and governors of provinces throughout the Empire that at their discretion they demand of all who may be accused of the Christian superstition that they burn incense to my likeness, by which act they will show their respect—not indeed to me, who am no better than other men—but to the majesty of the Empire."

He then went on: "In virtue of this authority, I command that you burn incense to the divine Trajan."

"If I must choose between two masters, I cannot doubt to prefer the Master who is in heaven. I refuse to burn incense."

"You are condemned of treason out of your own mouth," said the Governor.

"Nevertheless," returned the old man, resolute, like St. Paul, in asserting all lawful rights, "nevertheless, I appeal unto Cæsar."

"The appeal is allowed," said Pliny, "though I doubt whether it will much avail you."

The next prisoner called upon to answer was the old knight Antistius. The course of questions and answers was nearly the same as that which had been already described. The courage of Antistius faltered as little as that of his teacher and spiritual guide had done. From these two the infection of courage spread to the rest. Not one of the first batch of prisoners proved weak or faithless. They were, indeed, the most zealous, the most devoted, of the community—its chiefs and leaders, and they showed themselves worthy of their place.

But when the miscellaneous multitude that had been collected on the strength of the informations sent in to the Governor came to answer for themselves, all did not meet the test as well. Some had practically ceased to belong to the Church for many years; some had been excluded from it for conduct inconsistent with their profession; others had never belonged to it except in name—some passing fancy had attracted them, but they had shrunk back from the self-denial, the discipline, the strictly temperate rule of life which had been demanded of them. These had no difficulty in performing the acts enjoined upon them by the Governor. They threw the incense on the coals that were burning in the brazier with a careless gesture, repeating indifferently as they did so the formula: "Honour and worship to the divine Trajan and to all the gods who protect the city and Empire of Rome." They were almost as indifferent when they went on to satisfy the second test imposed upon them, and to curse the name of Christ. But these careless or reckless apostates—if they are to be so called—were but few in number. Many were reluctant to perform the idolatrous acts enjoined upon them; many shrank still more from the blasphemy which they were constrained to utter. The young Phrygian slave who has been described as accusing Verus to the Church was one of those whose courage failed them in this hour of trial. His was a weak nature, which curiously exemplified the famous saying in the "Odyssey"—that he who takes from a man his freedom, takes from him also half his manhood. Perhaps a finer temper would have disdained to play the part of the informer, even though this was done neither for revenge nor gain, but simply to serve (as he thought) the cause of the Church. Whatever the cause, he had a grievous fall, which Verus, of course, watched with malignant pleasure. At first it seemed as if his courage would hold out. When he was called upon to answer, he stood erect and answered with a firm voice, though his face was deadly pale and his limb could seem to tremble.

"Are you of the people who call themselves Christians?" asked the Governor.

"I am," said the young man.

"You make that answer deliberately, and after reflection? Take time to consider."

The poor creature seemed to feel that reflection would hardly serve to confirm his resolution, and he answered at once, "I do."

"The accused has confessed his crime. Let him be removed and dealt with after the manner of slaves."

When he heard these words a terrible vision of the punishment which they implied flashed across the young man's vision. He had seen a fellow-slave crucified a few days before. It was the wretched Lycus, the cupbearer, whose place he had taken on the memorable occasion of the banquet at which Verus was present. Sosicles, his master, had found that he had been guilty of a long career of thefts, and, enraged because the property stolen was lost beyond recovery, had pitilessly ordered him to the cross. From early dawn till late in the evening—when a feeling of weariness, rather than of compassion, had made Sosicles put an end to his sufferings—he had hung in torture. I would not describe those long hours of agony, even if I could. The young Phrygian had witnessed them. His master had compelled him to be present during the greater part of the day. "Go and see what your accursed folly may bring you to. It was, you tell me, your Master's fate—this Christus whom you are mad enough to worship; and it will be yours unless you take good heed. Judge for yourself how you would like it."

Sosicles spoke out of a certain regard—selfish, indeed, but still genuine—for the young man. He was diligent, sober, honest, and it would, he thought, be a grievous pity to lose him for some hare-brained fancy; and lose him he would to a certainty if this threatened movement against the Christians should come to anything.

It seemed now as if his worldly wisdom was not to fail of its effect. The terror of that thought, the horrors of the scene—every one of which memory seemed to bring up before the young man in a moment, and that with a hideous fidelity—overpowered him. "Hold, my lord," he cried, "I have reconsidered; I will obey your Excellency's command and offer the incense."

He took the pinch of incense from the plate and threw it on the fire, muttering as he did so the prescribed formula of words.

"You are wise in time," said the Governor; "you may stand down. Take heed that you do not repeat this folly, or it will not go so easily with you."

"May I speak, my lord?" said Verus, who saw with rage and disgust that his promised revenge was slipping out of his grasp.

"Speak on," said Pliny, who loathed the man, but could not refuse his request.

"Your lordship is aware that many who do not refuse to burn incense are unwilling to curse the name of their Master, as they call Him. I submit that the more effectual test should be applied to the accused."

"Let it be so," said the Governor.

One of the clerks of the court read out a formula which the wretched young man was to repeat after him. He began—

"I, having been accused of impiety and of neglect of the ancient gods, and of following after strange superstitions, hereby curse as a malefactor and deceiver——"

He had gone so far, and had now come to the holy name. Then he halted. In an agony of fear and doubt he looked round the court. All eyes were upon him. Stern reproach was in the looks of those who had witnessed their confession and had not failed. No face wore a sterner regard than that of Rhoda. It was pale and wasted; for the shock of the torture, though this had not been carried to any grievous extent, had sorely tried her sensitive frame. But this gave a more terrible fierceness to the fire of righteous indignation which seemed almost literally to blaze from her eyes. As the young Phrygian shrank from this scorching gaze, he met the gentle, pitying, appealing look of Cleoné. The girl was not one of those who are insensible to fear. Rhoda was an enthusiast who, as we sometimes read of martyrs of the more heroic mould, would have found a positive rapture of pleasure in the pain endured for conscience' sake. Cleoné was a delicate, sensitive woman, who had a natural shrinking from pain, but yet could nerve herself to bear it. She could sympathize with the poor young Phrygian's dread. Though she had never seen a sufferer on the cross, her vivid imagination helped her to realize its agony, and she pitied more than she abhorred the weakness which made him shrink from it. That look of pity saved him.

"Ah!" he thought to himself, "that was the way in which the Master looked at Peter when he had denied Him. I have denied Him, too; but Peter found a place of repentance, and so may I."

He turned boldly to the Governor. "No! I will not curse Him who has blessed me so often. I have sinned grievously in burning incense to that idol"—and he pointed as he spoke to the image of the Emperor—"but I will not add to my sin the burden of this intolerable iniquity."

"Ah!" whispered Tacitus to the Governor, "I have always heard that the genuine Christian stops short at this."

"Let the law have its course with the accused," said the Governor.

"Ah! my friend," said Verus to himself in a savage whisper, "you will not go interfering again with a gentleman's amusements."

"A curse on the obstinate villain!" muttered Sosicles, his master; "there go twenty-five minæ as good as lost, except I can get some compensation out of the Government. What business is it of theirs what the man believes? He belongs to me."

The young Phrygian's repentance seemed to give new boldness to all that remained to be examined. There were no more cases of apostasy.

The result of the day's proceedings was the condemnation of a crowd so numerous that they Governor was fairly staggered by the difficulty of having to deal with it. A few who could plead Roman citizenship were reserved for the judgment of the Emperor; but there remained many—both free persons and slaves—with whom it was his own duty to deal. To execute them all would be to order something like a massacre. Such severity might defeat its own object, for it might cause a reaction in favor of the Christians. Pliny's caution, not to speak of his humanity, made him shrink from incurring such a risk. He resolved to consult the Emperor by letter on the course which he ought to pursue. Till the answer should arrive, the condemned were to be shut in prison. The common gaol of Nicæa was not large enough to receive so many inmates, and many of the prisoners had to be sent to private houses, whose owners were to be held responsible for their safe custody. Rhoda and Cleoné were among those who were thus disposed of. The Governor was too humane and right-feeling to allow two young women so carefully nurtured to be exposed to the horrors of a gaol. They were committed to the care of Lucilius, whom the reader will remember to have been one of the conspirators who set on foot the movement against the Christians. The man, though hard and greedy for money, had a fair character for respectability; and his wife, as the Governor happened to know, was an amiable woman—much too good for her miserable husband.

11

THE HOUSE OF LUCILIUS

IT was a house of trouble into which the two sisters were thus brought. The only child of Lucilius was prostrated with a fever which had for some time been epidemic in Nicæa. He was a promising lad of sixteen, whose fine, generous, temper curiously contrasted with the mean and ignoble character of his father. For the last year or so, indeed,—since he had begun to be aware of what the outside world thought about the man whom as a son he was bound to respect—this contrast had troubled him much; and he had felt acutely the unhappiness of his home. His mother—sweet-tempered and gentle as she was, and carrying wifely obedience to the very verge of what duty enjoined—had a conscience that would not allow her to see wrong done without a protest. She would put up with any privation for herself; but to see her child stinted in what was necessary for his health, or the household slaves starved or half-poisoned with unwholesome food, was a thing that she could not endure in silence. Painful scenes became, in consequence, more and more frequent in the family. Lucilius's miserly habits grew upon him, as such habits will grow; and the gentle protests of his wife were met with furious anger, sometimes even with actual violence. These experiences were nothing less than agony to the son's sensitive temper. He loved his mother with his whole heart; he would fain have loved his father. In the old days, before the ruling passion had so mastered the man's being, his child was the one thing for which he cared; and even now the feeling was not wholly lost. If the miser had a soft spot in his heart—one not quite crusted over with the hardness of avarice—it was in his regard for his only child. Now and then he would show some tenderness for the boy; once or twice, by some tremendous effort of the will, he would even loosen his purse strings to buy something that would please him. It was curiously characteristic of the man's ruling vice that he found it easier to purchase for him some useless ornament than to relax the niggardly rules of his household expenditure. He would give the lad a costly jewel, and yet allow him to pine for the want of good and sufficient food. Possibly this kind of gift gratified his vanity; it may be—for there are no depths of meanness to which avarice will not descend—he could not help remembering that the good food was a perishable commodity, while the jewel represented a permanent value, and, in fact, was only property in another shape.

It can easily be imagined that these causes told, directly and indirectly, upon a constitution that had never been very strong, and that the fever found in the younger Lucilius a victim dangerously ready to succumb to its attack. The early symptoms of the disease had not passed unnoticed by the mother, and she had implored her husband to call in at once the assistance of a physician. Of course he refused. He had trained himself not to believe in the existence of anything that necessitated the expenditure of money, and he wilfully shut his eyes to indications which were manifest enough to every one else. In two or three days' time this self-deception ceased to be possible. The father had refused to notice—though not, we may believe, without some stifled misgivings—the flushed cheeks, the frequent cough, and the failing appetite; but when the lad could not rise from his bed, and when the ravings of delirium were heard outside the door of the boy's chamber, he could not ignore any longer the presence of disease. Then the physician was sent for in hot haste.

Dioscorides was a Greek who claimed to belong to what may be called the physician caste of the ancient world, the Asclepids, who traced their descent to Æsculapius, the god of healing, himself. For nearly fifty years he had the principal practice of Nicæa; his experience was vast, his skill and readiness of resource never failed him. It was these—rather than any traditional secrets of methods and remedies, such as popular report credited him with—that made him extraordinarily successful. He was an old man, whose face seemed to show at once much firmness and much benevolence. To his patients he was kindness and gentleness itself. He neglected nothing that could please, or even humour them. A modern practitioner of the healing art would perhaps smile at the extraordinary care with which he would prepare himself for a visit to a patient. His long white hair was always carefully combed and delicately perfumed; his robes were beautifully clean. "We must please," he would say, "a sick man's senses as much as we can. Nothing ought to be neglected that can minister to that end."

But while he was gentle, he was firm when firmness was needed. Pretences of every kind met with no sort of mercy from him. If a fine lady, whose only real malady was indolence, sent for him, she was sure to hear the truth without any attempt at disguise. He was no fashionable physician, making a profit out of the whims and fancies of idleness and luxury. "You work too little; you eat and drink too much," was the homely formula with which he described the ailments of these imaginary invalids. If they dismissed him, as they were apt to do in the first annoyance of hearing an unwelcome truth, he accepted the dismissal with a smile. His practice was too large and lucrative to make him care for the loss of this or that patient; and he knew perfectly well that, when any serious cause occurred, he would be sent for again.

Lucilius, whose character and habits were perfectly well known to him, was, of course, not going to escape without hearing some truth from his lips.

"You should have sent for me," he said, "three days ago."

"I did not think that there was any need," said the father, in a faltering voice. His conscience had begun to prick him; and he knew, too, that all disguises would be useless with the clear-sighted, plain-speaking Dioscorides.

"Nonsense, man!" answered the physician, sharply. "You can see, you can hear! You must have heard the lad cough; you must have seen him wasting before your eyes! Don't tell me you didn't think there was any need. The truth is that you shut your eyes and ears because you were afraid of the fees. Now I am very much afraid that it is too late!"

"Oh! sir, don't say so," cried the wretched man, whose heart, hardened as it was with the most deadening of all vices, was touched by the danger of his son—"don't say so. I will spare nothing; save him, and you shall name your own fee."

"Not all the gold in the world," returned the physician, "can purchase the three days that have been lost; but I will do all I can for the lad and his mother. Only the gods in heaven know," he added in a half-audible aside, "how such a woman came to marry such a mean hound—only there is no knowing the follies of women—and how such a father came to have such a son." He went on, turning to Lucilius, "The only chance for the boy now is the best of nursing. His mother is not strong enough; besides, she is too anxious. As a rule I don't believe in mothers' nursing; they are apt to lose their heads. And hired nursing is seldom much good either," went on the old man, talking to himself; "just what's in the letter of the bond, and no more; must have their so many hours' rest, and so forth; all for themselves and nothing for the patient. Of course there are exceptions, but I can't think of any one who is available just at this moment. Now, if you could get one of those two young women, Rhoda or Cleoné, or both of them—for it will be more than one can well manage—it would be perfect; they would do the thing for love, and yet not be too anxious. But then they have been mixed up in this foolish business of the Christians, and there is no getting at them, I suppose."

"By good fortune, sir," Lucilius interrupted at this moment, "the two young women are to be put in my keeping, pending the arrival of the Emperor's letter."

"Thank the gods for your good fortune," cried the old physician in his delight; "if anything can save the lad, it will be their nursing. I have had some opportunities for observing it, and it is simply perfect. When do they come?"

"I had notice that they would be delivered to my hands at noon," answered Lucilius.

"That will give me time," said the physician, "to visit two or three other patients. I will return and give them my instructions; and, mind, in case I should not see you again, they must have every thing they ask for."

This, then, was the state of things which the two prisoners found on their arrival at the house of Lucilius. They threw themselves into the duty which they found so strangely ready to their hand with wonderful energy, though Rhoda was more fit to be nursed than to nurse. With a touching humility and sacrifice of personal feeling, the mother gave up her charge into their hands. To be allowed to help, to do something for the darling of her heart, was all that she asked. Even this consolation she was ready to give up if she thought that the service it was such a delight to render was better given by another.

But when all their efforts seemed unavailing, when the lad grew weaker every day, and the delirium left fewer and fewer lucid intervals, the behaviour of the mother underwent a curious change—all the more curious when it was contrasted with the altered demeanour of her husband. Something had found its way at last to the cold heart of the miser; disappointed ambition had something to do with it. He had wanted to give his family such rank as could be acquired by wealth, and wealth had about as much power in Bithynia in the days of Trajan as it has in London in the days of Victoria. But what if the son for whom he was saving—and he constantly salved his conscience for mean or unprincipled acts by repeating to himself at all his savings were for his son—what if is son should die? Curiously mixed up with this meaner motive was a genuine love for his child. For the time, at least, the man's hard nature was broken through. His purse was opened now without reluctance to purchase anything that the sick lad could need. He would wait with humble patience outside the door of the sick-chamber for the latest news. The sisters naturally thought that this manifest softening of the heart would have brought him nearer to his wife; but they were astonished to see that the woman, for all the gentleness of her nature, shrank more and more from him, and seemed to feel no comfort in his sympathy, and not to be touched by his manifest grief. Rhoda was the unwilling witness of a painful scene in which this growing alienation seemed to culminate. Made desperate by the increasing peril which threatened his son's life—and, indeed, Dioscorides himself, the most hopeful as he was the most skilful of his profession, had begun to give up hope— the wretched man turned, by way of a last resource, to the help of heavenly powers. He tried to persuade himself that it might not be altogether unavailing; he could anyhow believe that it would do no harm to appeal to it. This idea he communicated to his wife in the presence of the elder of the two sisters. The physician was paying one of his visits, and Cleoné was in the room to hear the instructions as to what was to be done till he should come again. Lucilius and his wife, with Rhoda, were in an adjoining chamber.

"Shall we offer a sacrifice for our poor boy?" he asked.

Then the gentle woman's wrath fairly blazed out. Rhoda watched the explosion with such astonishment as one might feel were a lamb to show the ferocity of a tiger.

"You," she cried, "you offer sacrifice! Will the righteous gods listen to you? Will you even dare to touch their altars with your murderous hands? This is their judgment upon you. I knew it would come sooner or later. I had hoped that it would not be till I had got my release from the horrible bond that ties me to you. But the gods do not suffer me to escape, for I, too, am guilty. And now the stroke has fallen on you and on me!"

A terrible fascination seemed to keep the girl's yes fixed on the face of Lucilius as the woman, who seemed positively transfigured by her rage, poured out this stream of reproaches on him. At first it expressed keen astonishment, then a dreadful look of fear seemed to creep over it. Once and again he opened his lips, as if he would have spoken, but no sound came forth from them.

"Be silent—be silent," at last he managed to utter, and so turned and staggered out of the room.

12

A MARTYR'S TESTIMONY

THE young Lucilius was still hovering between life and death when the long-expected answer from the Emperor arrived at Nicæa. It was exactly the document that any one acquainted with the character of Trajan might have expected. Above all things he was a soldier, and had a soldier's regard for discipline and obedience. Where these were concerned he was inflexible.

Certain forms of worship were sanctioned by the State; all others were forbidden. Any one who adhered to these forbidden rites and refused, when called upon, to abandon them, was breaking down the established order of things, and must be punished. He might believe what he liked in his own heart—with belief the State had nothing to do—but in practice he must conform to certain rules. Refusal was an act of rebellion; the thing might be the merest trifle in itself, but the principle concerned was at the foundation of all order.

The practical application was perfectly simple. Those who had acknowledged themselves to be Christians, and persisted in the acknowledgment, were to be punished. But the offence was of such a kind that every loophole should be left by which the accused might escape, so long as the principle remained unimpaired. These were not a set of criminals whom it would be desirable to bring into the grasp of the law, by stopping every way of escape. On the contrary, ways of escape must be made easy and multiplied for them. The simple denial of any one that he belonged to the society of Christians was to be accepted. There was to be no question about the time to which the denial referred, so that it at least referred to the present. If a man affirmed, "I have ceased to be a Christian," there was to be no curious inquiry as to when his withdrawal took place.

But the most practically important direction in the Emperor's rescript referred to the anonymous informations. All proceedings founded on them were to be annulled. Roman law took no cognisance of such things; and persons accused under them were to be treated as if their names had never come before the court. The immediate result of this order was a release of a number of prisoners. Of the two Roman citizens who had appealed to Cæsar, one—the Elder, Anicetus—was sent back into the province. The Emperor had heard his cause, and condemned him. The Governor was to deal with him on the spot, where the spectacle of his punishment might act as a salutary deterrent to his followers. The old knight, Antistius, by a merciful ordering of Providence, had passed beyond the reach of his judges. On the morning of the day on which he was to appear before the tribunal of Cæsar he had been found dead in his bed.

The Governor's first duty, on the reassembling of the court, was to deal with the prisoner who had been thus remitted to him. The Elder was placed before the tribunal, and the Governor addressed him—

"Anicetus, or (as I should rather call you by the Roman name which, however unworthily, you bear) Lucius Cornelius: the Emperor, having heard you on your appeal and confirmed the sentence which was here passed upon you, has remitted you to my jurisdiction, thinking it well that you should suffer the penalty of your misdeeds in the same place wherein you have committed them. I should do no wrong were I, without further parley, to hand you over to the executioner. Nevertheless, I am persuaded that, in the great clemency of our gracious lord and Emperor, Trajan Augustus, he will approve my offering you yet another opportunity of repentance. Are you willing to renounce, now, at the last moment, this odious superstition which you have been convicted of holding, against the laws of the Senate and People of Rome?"

"For your clemency," said the Elder, in reply, "I heartily thank both Trajan Augustus and yourself, most excellent Plinius. Yet, were I to accept it on the conditions which you offer, I should be casting away that which, for my whole life, I have held most precious. That which you call an odious superstition I do verily believe to be a truth worthy of all love and honour. The laws of the Senate and People of Rome I have ever most scrupulously obeyed, and to the Emperor I have ever been faithful and loyal. But there are laws to which I am yet more bound, and a Master whom I must prefer even to Augustus himself. But these things you have heard already, nor is there any need that I should repeat them. Let me not waste your time any further, nor do you delay to give me that which I hold to be more precious than all other things—the crown of martyrdom."

The executioner was summoned into court, and took his place in front of the tribunal. The Governor then pronounced his formal sentence—

"In virtue of the power of life and death specially delegated to me in the case of the citizen Lucius Cornelius (commonly called Anicetus) by our Lord Trajan Augustus, I hereby hand over to you the body of the said Lucius Cornelius. Take him to the third milestone on the road to Nicomedia, and there strike off his head with the axe. In consideration of his blameless life, I grant to him, as a special favour, that he be neither blindfolded nor bound. Of this sentence let there be immediate execution, of which execution I require that testimony be given me before sunset this day."

The court was adjourned till the next day, when the remainder of the prisoners would be dealt with. An interval of two hours was conceded to the condemned man. This the Governor's humanity permitted him to spend with his fellow-prisoners.

Of earthly ties he had none. His wife—for in those days it was held a duty, as the Eastern Church still holds it, for a Christian minister to be a husband—had entered into her rest some two years before. His marriage had been childless, and his brothers and sisters had predeceased him. Hence he could give up the time that had been allowed him to comforting and strengthening his brethren and sisters in the faith.

To Cleon, the young Phrygian slave who had fallen, and so manfully recovered his fall, he was especially tender. The unhappy youth was overwhelmed with shame and remorse.

"I have denied Him! I have denied Him!" he would go on repeating day after day, from morning till evening, and nothing that his fellow-prisoners could urge seemed to give him any comfort.

Anicetus was one of those who were accustomed to express somewhat stern views about the sin of the lapsi (those who fell away), but this was not a case in which he could insist on them. He even felt that to do so might be to place a fatal stumbling-block in the way of an imperilled soul. If this poor wretch was left in this despairing mood, he might even fall into the more deadly sin from which he had once been rescued.

"My son," were his parting words to the unhappy Cleon, "my son, listen to me, not only as to him whom God has entrusted with the charge of your soul, but as one to whom He has given the great honour of witnessing for His truth in this place. You have sinned, but God has forgiven you, even as He forgave the blessed Peter. God pardon you; I pardon you in the name of the brethren."

He laid his hands upon the young man's head, and pronounced the solemn words of forgiveness. That finished, he gave him the kiss of peace, and so took the fallen back into the brotherhood of Christ.

We shall not have occasion to speak of the young slave again. Let it be sufficient to say that he suffered the next day the cruel death of crucifixion with an exemplary courage and patience. His agony, however, was not protracted as long as it was in the case of some sufferers, for the Governor, who had been struck with the real heroism with which he had struggled against the weakness of a timorous nature, gave instructions to the centurion in charge that death should be hastened with a spear-thrust.

To return to Anicetus. His solemn declaration of forgiveness to the penitent Phrygian was but just spoken when the presence of the executioner was announced.

"I am ready," he said to the apparitor who summoned him. Then turning to his fellow-prisoners, he stretched out his hands: "The blessing of the Father, the Son, and the Holy Ghost be upon you. Pray for me, and for yourselves, that we may be faithful and steadfast to the end. So shall we be together in Paradise."

The procession of death moved through the city. In front was a guard of half a century of soldiers. They were armed with swords only, and wore no armour beyond their helmets. Then came the executioner, carrying his axe with the edge turned towards the condemned man, who had also a soldier fully armed on either side. The remainder of the century marched behind him. A vast concourse of all ages followed. No man was better known to the poor of the city of Nicæa, and no one certainly more beloved than Anicetus. He had fulfilled to the utmost the apostolic precept, "Do good unto all men," putting less stress, perhaps, than some of his brethren thought right, on the words that follow, "especially unto them that are of the household of faith." It was no idle curiosity, therefore, that brought this great crowd to see him die. To judge from their dress, one would have said that they came from the rabble of the city; but they followed with a silence and an order that would not have misbecome the funeral of the first citizen of the place.

At the spot appointed for the execution there was an open space of about an acre in extent. The milestone stood where four roads met, and close to it, as marking where the territory of Nicæa touched that of a neighbouring township, stood one of the statues of the god Terminus, the boundary-marker, a roughly hewn pedestal of granite, surmounted with a human bust of the rudest shaping. In old time it had been an object of reverence, and had been daily adorned with fresh garlands of flowers or evergreens, according as the season served. Two or three of these still hung from it, but they were dry and withered, and the decaying fragments of others, which no one had taken the pains to clear away, lay at the base of the pedestal; while the pedestal itself had long leaned somewhat out of the perpendicular. It was a type of the neglect into which the old worship was everywhere falling. Possibly this was the motive that made the Governor choose the spot as the place of execution.

The block was placed close to the pedestal. The soldiers drew a cordon round it, but as the ground rose somewhat on all sides, this did not shut out the view from the crowd which thronged the whole of the open space. The centurion in command had forbidden the condemned man to address the spectators, and Anicetus, always obedient to lawful commands, so that they did not trench on higher duties, did not attempt to speak. He contented himself with stretching out his hands in a mute gesture of blessing. Many of those who could see him bowed their heads in reverence, and, dangerous as it was to show anything like sympathy with the faith of the sufferer, some even fell upon their knees. All kept a silence which was almost terrible in its depth and intensity. Then, after a pause, which seemed to the strained attention of the crowd to last for hours, the executioner raised his axe and struck. It was a strong and skilful blow, nor was there any need to repeat it. The head of the martyr fell upon the ground, and the blood, spouting out in a torrent, drenched the pedestal of the god.

And then followed one of those strange occurrences which we may or may not call miracles, but which are certainly signs; so full are they of meaning, and not the less truly signs because they come from causes strictly natural. The statue of the boundary-god had been leaning, as has been said, for some time out of the perpendicular, and the piety of the two townships, whose borders it marked, had not been active enough to restore it. Any one might have known that but a little impulse would be sufficient to overthrow it; and this impulse was given by the slight shock of an earthquake at the very moment when the martyr's blood spurted on the pedestal. The half-suppressed groan which had followed when the headsman's axe was seen or heard to fall was checked; first, by the sensation of terror as the spectators felt the ground reel, as it were, under their feet, and then by awe as the statue of the god was observed first to totter and then to fall.

No one in all that great assembly was so dull as not to read something of the future when this ancient landmark—symbol as it was held to be of all that was most stable—was removed, as it were, from its place by the touch of the martyr's blood. If the champions of the old faith had thought to advance their cause by that day's spectacle, they had signally failed. The "senseless earth," as the philosophers called it, had seemed to speak against them, and its voice had found its way into many hearts. Seldom has the saying been proved more true than it was that day, that "the blood of martyrs is the seed of the Church."

It was an incidental result of this strange event that the friends of Anicetus were allowed, without hindrance, to take possession of his remains. Commonly the authorities took care to dispose of them otherwise. In the consternation that followed the fall of the statue this care was forgotten, and the Elder's body was quietly removed, and accorded Christian burial.

13

A DISCOVERY

"THE mills of God," says an old writer, "grind slowly, but they grind exceeding small;" and Lucilius was beginning to find out this truth for himself. Again and again he bitterly reproached himself for lending his help to the conspiracy which had been hatched in the wine-shop of Theron. So far, none of the gains that he had expected to flow in from the confiscated estates had reached his coffers. Antistius, who was a really wealthy man, had died (as has been said) in Rome, and it was a doubtful point who would benefit by his property. Would it go where the appeal had been decided—that is, in the Capital—or where he had been condemned in the first instance? The provincial claimant might have the better right in law, but Lucilius knew perfectly well that when such rights came to collision with the demands of the Imperial purse, they were pretty sure to go to the wall. Anicetus had been far too generous in his lifetime to leave anything behind him after his death. Most of the richer among the accused had saved their properties as well as their lives by denying their faith. In short, the speculation, so far, had been a failure.

On the other hand, the prospect at home grew darker and darker. Whatever feeling his long-indulged habit of avarice had left him was centred in his son, and this son's life was trembling in the balance. At first it had seemed a lucky chance that brought the two sisters to his house. They had kept the boy alive. Latterly, Rhoda's increasing weakness had compelled her to give up her share in the nursing, and Cleoné had assumed the whole.

She was simply indispensable to the boy. It was from her hand only that he would take food or drink. When his delirium was at its worst, it was her hand that soothed and quieted him. But if she had to leave him, it would have been better that she had never come.

The old physician was furious at the thought. All his cases interested him deeply, but in this he was especially wrapt up. Never had he fought against disease more pertinaciously and more skilfully, and never had he been more ably helped by the physician's best ally, a good nurse. It was simply maddening to him to have this assistance removed, for the loss meant defeat. He cursed with impartial rage every one concerned in the matter: the busybodies who had stirred up the movement against the Christians; the foolish obstinacy—for so he described it—which made these people cling to their absurd superstition.

But nothing could be done. The Emperor's commands had to be executed, and all persons who had confessed their adherence to the Christian faith would have to be dealt with according to law. Among these were the two sisters. A formal demand was made by the officials upon Lucilius for their surrender, and he had no alternative but to submit. They were included in the company of prisoners arraigned before the Governor's tribunal on the day that followed the execution of Anicetus. Lucilius was among the crowd of spectators which thronged the court-house and awaited the result with feelings of despair.

Nothing could save the sisters. He knew them too well to have the least hope that they would renounce their faith to save their lives. A vague suggestion to that effect on which he had once ventured during the time of their sojourn in his house had been received by Cleoné with a scorn that brought conviction to his mind. Their condemnation, then, was certain.

Hard-hearted as he was, he could not contemplate this result with indifference. They had lived in his house for some weeks. Their grace and goodness, seen in the close intercourse of family life, had touched him as he had never dreamt of being touched, and he shuddered at the thought of their being handed over to the shame and torture of the slave's death.

And then there was the thought of his son. Even if he were to battle through the disease without the help of his nurse, what would be the result when he heard, as hear he must, of the horrible fate which had overtaken her? The wretched man groaned aloud when he thought of what the future had in store for him.

He was roused from the stupor of despair into which he had fallen by the voice of the court-crier calling aloud the names of Rhoda and Cleoné. Rhoda was described as an ancilla, i.e., a female slave, and as a deaconess attached to a certain unlawful society which called itself by the name of Christus. Cleoné was also described as being of servile condition.

When the clerk of the court had finished reading what we may call the indictment, the Governor addressed the prisoners. "The clemency of our most gracious lord and master, Trajan Augustus, has ordered that even for the most obstinate offenders there should be provided a place of repentance, if only, even at the last moment, they will submit themselves to lawful authority, and renounce their obstinate adherence to a mischievous superstition. Therefore I call upon you, Rhoda, for the last time. Are you willing to burn incense to the statue of the divine Trajan, and to curse this Christus, whom you superstitiously and rebelliously have honoured as a God?"

Rhoda had remained seated during the proceedings. Her weakness did not permit her to stand with the rest of the prisoners. She now rose, and confronted the Governor. Fear she had never known; and, for the moment, her bodily strength seemed to have been restored to her.

"I thank the Emperor," she said, in a voice which never faltered for a moment, "for the clemency which he offers, though I cannot but refuse the conditions. For him, as our ruler appointed by God, I pray all blessings; and especially light, that he may discern the truth. Such honour as a man may receive, I willingly pay; more I refuse; for it is written, 'Thou shalt worship the Lord thy God, and Him only shalt thou serve.' That I should blaspheme my Lord and Saviour is a thing too monstrous to be thought, much more spoken."

"What say you, Cleoné?" went on the Governor, addressing himself to the other sister.

"I am of one mind with my sister. I will not worship a man; neither will I blaspheme my God."

"Rhoda and Cleoné," said the Governor, "are condemned to suffer the punishment of death in such manner as is customary with those of servile condition."

At this moment a commotion was heard at the back of the court. The young Greek, Clitus, whose acquaintance we have already made in his character as Cleoné's suitor, made his way with difficulty through the crowd that besieged the door into the body of the chamber. He had just arrived in Nicæa, and his dress bore the marks of travel.

"My lord," he said, addressing the Governor, "is it permitted me to speak on a matter of urgency, which concerns the administration of justice in this matter, and especially the case of the two prisoners Rhoda and Cleoné?"

Rhoda, who had sunk again into her seat, seemed not to notice this interruption of the proceedings. But Cleoné turned an eager look upon the speaker. She had never seen or even heard of the young Greek since the day on which they had spoken together among the vines. She had striven to school herself into the persuasion that it was well that it should be so. He had spoken of love in days past, it was true, but all was now changed. He was a citizen of Rome, and had it not been proved that she was a slave? In any case, there was henceforth a hopeless separation between them. And then, what had she, a condemned woman, to do with thoughts of love? No, it was well that he had not attempted to hold any communication with her. It was only what prudence, and even duty, dictated—that he should keep aloof. So she had thought, or tried to think. Nevertheless, her heart gave a glad bound when she knew that, after all, he had not forgotten her; and the exalted look on her face, which showed how she had braced herself up to confess and suffer, changed to a softer and more tender expression as she listened to what he said.

"Speak on," said the Governor, "if you have anything of importance to engage the ear of the court."

The young Greek proceeded. "Your Excellency is aware that the two women, Rhoda and Cleoné, hitherto reputed daughters of one Bion and Rhoda his wife, were adjudged to be of servile condition on testimony by which it was proved that they were not in truth daughters of the said Bion, but were castaway children, adopted by him and his wife.

"I have now to bring under your Excellency's notice the terms of an Imperial rescript quoted by yourself in this court last December, as settling a certain question concerning the condition of exposed children submitted by you to the Emperor. These terms were in substance as follows—your Excellency will correct me if I am wrong, but I took them down in writing at the time, as seeming to me to be of great importance:—'If it should be proved that children so exposed were born of free parents, their free condition shall not be held to have been impaired by such exposure.' This, my lord, is exactly what I am now prepared to prove of the two women Rhoda and Cleoné. And first I will, with your permission, produce the witness on whose testimony I chiefly rely, though indeed it can easily be confirmed by other evidence."

"Inform the court of the name and condition of this witness. But it will promote the ends of justice if you will first inform us of your own proceedings in this case, and of how you were led to believe that our adjudications needed to be corrected."

"My lord," began the young advocate, "it must have occurred to you and to others who were present on the first day of the trial, as certainly it occurred to me, that nature had committed, if I may so speak, a strange freak when she ordered that maidens of an appearance so noble, so worthy of freedom, should be born of slaves."

"The thought was not unreasonable," said the Governor; "but such eccentricities are not unknown, and the evidence seemed to support the presumption."

"Further, my lord, I was aware that this nobility was not of appearance only, but of mind also and disposition, for I had been admitted into the home of Bion, the reputed father of the two, and know that none could be more worthy of respect and love."

Cleoné cast down her eyes, blushing to hear these praises from her lover's lips.

"But I will leave suppositions, my lord, and proceed to facts. I gathered from the evidence that there was a secret connected with the birth of these two children—that the only person who had been known to be cognisant of this secret was a certain nurse, and that this person was now deceased. It was also proved that, when about to die, she had refused to communicate the knowledge that she evidently possessed. The only hope that seemed to me to remain was, if I could discover that there had been some other person who had shared, or might be supposed likely to have shared, in this knowledge. I made many inquiries for such a person, and for a long time could hear of none. Her husband had been long dead. She had left no children behind her. But at last I heard from a woman of the same age, who is yet alive, that she had a brother who had been a slave in the city. All that I could learn about him was that he had suddenly disappeared from this neighbourhood; that some supposed that he had been drowned, but others doubted, seeing that his body had never been found. Here, then, my inquiries seemed to have an end.

"But now, my lord, listen to what followed. Your Excellency sent me on business, wholly unconnected with this matter, to a certain village on the borders of Phrygia. It was finished sooner than I had expected, and as I could not return till my horse had had a day's rest, I had some time to spare. I spent it in wandering about the downs which are above the village, and in the course of my walks I fell in with an old shepherd. The man interested me with his talk, which touched upon more things than such a man commonly knows. He happened to let fall something, from which I gathered that he knew this town. When I asked him a question about it, he seemed unwilling to speak. I pressed him. Something seemed to warn me that by chance, if there is such thing as chance, I had found the man whom I wanted."

"You are a student," interrupted the Governor, and you know doubtless how one of your historians speaks of an 'inspired chance.' It was that, if I remember right, which made the baby Cypselus smile in the face of the men who came to murder him. Chance, I take it, is an ordering of things which we do not understand, and we may well call it inspired. But go on."

"Well, my lord, as I said, I pressed him, and he told me that he knew this town well. And then he gave me the story of how he came to leave it. But as this story bears directly upon the matter in hand, I would suggest, with your permission, that you should hear it from the man's own lips."

The witness, who had been waiting outside in the charge of one of the officers of the court, was called in. His face, curiously seamed with lines and wrinkles beyond all counting, indicated an extreme old age; but it was an age that was still vigorous and green. His blue eyes were bright and piercing. His hair was abundant, and showed amidst the prevailing grey much of the auburn which had been its color in the days of his prime. His tall figure was but little bowed by years; and his broad shoulders and sinewy arm (the right of them left bare by his one-sleeved tunic) showed that he might still be a match for many a younger man.

It was evident that the scene into which he had been brought was wholly strange to him, and that he was not at all at his ease. He had stood nervously shifting his red Phrygian cap from one hand to another, while his eye roved restlessly over the crowded court.

"Tell us your name," said the Governor.

"My lord," said the man in Greek, "let me first implore your protection." The refinement of his voice and accent contrasted curiously with his uncultured look. In garb he was a rustic of the rustics; but it might be seen that he had once been a dweller in cities.

"You can speak without fear," said the Governor.

"I shall have to say that which may be brought up against myself.

It concerns years long past; but if the man against whom I offended still lives, he is not one of those who forgive."

"No one shall harm you if you will speak the truth. I promise it by the majesty of Augustus."

"More than twenty years ago I was steward in the household of a certain merchant in Nicæa."

"What was his name?" asked the Governor.

"With your permission, I will reserve this to the end of the story which I have to relate. I was a slave, but I had been well taught, and he trusted me with much of his business. I kept his accounts, and I knew much of his affairs. He was, at the time of which I speak, a man of about forty years of age. Five years before, he had married the only daughter of the merchant Lycophron of Nicomedia. Lycophron was reputed to be rich, and my master, who was very greedy after money, expected to inherit much wealth from him.

"Lycophron had given but a very small portion to his daughter on her marriage. This was a grievance with my master; but he hoped to have it made up to him. I have heard the two talking about it—they always spoke openly before me. ' Never mind,' the old man would say; 'there will be the more when you come to unseal the tablets, and by that time you will know how to use it and keep it better.' This was a joke of the old man's, for no man could make more of money, or cared less for spending it, than my master.

"Well, at the time of which I am speaking, news came that old Lycophron was dead, and my master started at once for Nicomedia. He was not very willing, for my mistress was then not very well. Three days after, he came back. He was in a furious rage, and broke out as soon as he saw me. 'Listen, Geta,' he said: 'that old villain has deceived me. He has not left so much as a single drachma behind him. His house was mortgaged; the very bed on which he died was pledged. When I came to open his will—for he had the impudence to leave a will, though there was nothing to dispose of—I found written in it—"The only possession of value that belongs to me I have already given away, to wit, my daughter Eubule. My son-in-law, who has now known for five years what a treasure he has found in her, will not be disappointed to know that I can give him nothing more." These were his very words. Yes; he palmed off his beggar's brat on me very cleverly. A treasure, indeed!'

"Just at this moment the nurse who had been attending on my mistress came into the room carrying two babies, one on each arm. Her face was wreathed in smiles, and she was so full of her own importance—as such women, I have observed, are wont to be—that she did not see what a state my master was in. 'Thank the gods, sir,' she said, 'who have given you two most beautiful daughters.'—'Curse them!' he began. By chance one of the children began to cry at the very moment, and the woman did not hear what he said. By the time she had quieted the baby he had recovered himself. He kissed the children, and went up to see his wife as soon as he was allowed to do so.

"Some days afterwards my mistress became very ill. Fever showed itself, and she became delirious. The children had to be taken from her, and brought up by a nurse. I think my master was getting reconciled to his disappointment, when, as bad luck would have it, he heard of another loss. This time it was his wife's brother had failed. He farmed some of the taxes of the province, and my master had become security for him. I heard him say to himself when he had read the letter that told him about it, 'This family will be my ruin.'

"That night, after I had been asleep about an hour, he woke me up. He looked very wild. I think his losses had half-crazed him. He was carrying a cradle, and the two babies were in it, lying head to feet, and sound asleep. 'Geta,' he said, 'these children will be my ruin. If they were boys, now—but how can a beggar like me keep two girls? You must put them out on the hill.'—'O master!' I said, 'not these beautiful babies!'—'It is better than strangling them,' he said.

"Well, I had scarcely a moment to think what was to be done. He looked as if he might do the poor things a mischief, so I made up my mind. 'Very well, master,' I said, 'it shall be done.'—'Their mother,' he said, 'knows nothing; perhaps never will know. Take them, and do it at once.' I got up and went out with the children. It was a stormy night, and raining in torrents. I was at my wits' end. Then a thought occurred to me. I had a sister, a nurse, living in the town; perhaps she might help me. I took the babies to her house, and told her the whole story.

" 'You have come in time,' she said; 'I know of a home for the dear little beauties. It is with one of the best couples in the world, but the gods have not given them any children.'—'So be it,' I said; 'but you must swear that you will never tell where they came from.' So she took an oath, and I left them there. But I did not dare to go back to my master. I ran away, leaving my hat and shoes on the river-side, to make people think that I had been drowned. I made my way to a village in Phrygia, and took up a shepherd's business, in which I had had some experience when I was young. There I was when this young lawyer found me."

"And now tell us your master's name," said the Governor.

The whole audience listened in breathless silence for his answer.

"My master's name was Lucilius."

14

A LETTER FROM TRAJAN

"IS this man Lucilius in court?" asked the Governor of one of the officials.

"I saw him this morning, my lord," said the person addressed.

"Crier, call Lucilius."

The crier called the name, but there was no answer. The wretched man had listened to the evidence of the slave with growing apprehension, which was soon changed into dismay. At first, indeed, he had wholly failed to recognise the man. The lapse of twenty years and more had of course made a great change in Geta's appearance. The old shepherd, tanned to an almost African hue by exposure to wind and sun, with his grizzled beard and moustache, and long, unkempt locks falling over his shoulders, and his roughly made garments of skin, was as different a figure as possible from the neat, well-dressed, confidential servant whom Lucilius had known in time past. Still, some vague indication of the voice, as soon as the man began to speak, had troubled him; and of course little room had been left to him for doubt as soon as the man began to tell his story.

Lucilius was not so heartless but that he had often thought with regret of the two beautiful girl babies whom he had put out to die.

The crime was indeed far too common in the ancient world to rouse the horror which it now excites. Indeed, it was a recognised practice. The fate of a new-born child was not considered to be fixed till the father by taking it up in his arms had signified his wish that it should be reared.

Still, the remembrance of that night's deed had troubled him. Prosperous days had soon come, and the losses which had infuriated him had been repaired. Then the grief of his wife, whom he loved with all the affection of which his nature was capable, had much troubled him. As a mere matter of domestic peace, her mourning for her lost darlings—though, as we shall see, she did not know of their actual fate—had destroyed all the comfort of his home. And for some years his home was childless. When, after an interval, a son was born, and the mother forgot something of her grief in the care which she lavished upon him, the father was stricken by a new fear—what if this child should be taken from him by way of retribution for the hard-heartedness with which he had treated his first-born? Every ailment of infancy and childhood had made him terribly anxious ; and he watched over the boy who was to carry out his ambitions with an apprehension which conscience never allowed him to set free.

As the lad grew up these fears had fallen into the background. But we have seen how they had of late been revived, and, it seemed, justified. The shepherd's story made them more intense than ever, while it added a new horror. It was a hideous thought that he should have helped to doom his own daughters to torture and death; and he saw what would be the end when his son should know of it. The wretched man waited in court till he had heard enough to banish all doubt from his mind, and then hurried home, half expecting as he came near the house to hear the lamentations for the newly dead.

As a matter of fact, no change had taken place in the condition of the invalid. He had woke two or three times since the departure of Cleoné, but never so thoroughly as to become aware of her absence. He had taken mechanically from his mother's hand the nourishment offered him, and had almost instantly fallen asleep. The physician had just paid his morning visit, and was more hopeful. For the present at least the lad was doing well. But when the explanation had to be made, that was another matter altogether.

Lucilius entered the sick boy's chamber with a silent step. His wife took no notice of his coming; but when he stood fronting her on the opposite side of the bed, and she could not help seeing his face, her woman's heart was touched by its inexpressible misery. She went round to his side, and laid her hand with a caressing gesture on his arm.

"What ails you, my husband?" she said. "Our darling, I hope, is doing well. The good Dioscorides speaks well of him."

He made no answer, but, falling on his knees beside the bed, buried his face in the coverlet. She could see his body shaken with silent and tearless sobs. At last he managed to articulate: "Call Manto"—Manto was an old and trustworthy servant who had been long a member of the household—"and let her watch for a while. I have something to tell you."

When Manto had obeyed the summons, Lucilius, who seemed to have become almost helpless, was led by his wife into an adjoining chamber.

Then, in a voice broken by sobs and tears, he told the miserable story.

He had scarcely finished when an official arrived from the Governor's court, bringing a summons for his attendance.

The wretched man rose from his seat as if to obey. But the limit of his strength and endurance had been reached, and he fell swooning upon the floor. Before long he was restored to partial consciousness; but it was evident that his attendance at the court was out of the question. In fact, he was suffering from a slight shock of paralysis.

"Let me go instead of him," said the wife. "I can at least tell what I know, and you can examine him when he is fit to answer."

Accordingly, after giving directions to Manto as to what was to be done for the patient during her absence, she accompanied the official to the court.

It was not much that she had to say; but, so far as it went, it confirmed the shepherd's story.

"I became the mother of two female children," she said, "on the fourteenth of May, twenty-one years ago. They were born alive, and were healthy and strong. I nursed them for fourteen days, as far as I can remember. Then I fell ill of a fever, and they had to be taken from me. I remember seeing them several times in the day for two or three days afterwards; then I knew nothing more. When I recovered my senses they were gone. It was then nearly the end of June. My husband told me that they were dead."

"Had you any doubt whether he was telling you the truth?" asked the Governor.

"I had none. Why should I? And when we were reckoning up our expenses at the end of the year, I found a paper which seemed to show the sum paid for the funeral."

"Do you remember the slave Geta?"

"Yes; I remember him. My husband said that he had been drowned. Some articles of his clothing were found by the river."

"Have you had any suspicion at all up to this time?"

"Lately I have had. Since my son has been ill, my husband has been much troubled in mind. He has talked in his sleep; and he said the same things over and over again, till I could not choose but heed them. 'Why did I kill them? Why did I kill them?' 'Geta, Geta, bring them back!' and 'Childless! Childless!' These were the things that he repeated. I put them together till I began to suspect that there had been some foul play. And then I remembered some words the old woman, Geta's sister, had said."

"And have you anything else to say?"

"Nothing, my lord, except that within the last hour my husband has confessed to me the whole."

"Why is he not here?"

"He is paralysed."

Here the poor woman, who had given her evidence with extraordinary firmness and self-possession, utterly broke down.

The Governor took but little time to consider his decision. It was to this effect:—

"The legal proof in this case is not complete, for it needs the formally attested confession of the man Lucilius. Substantially, however, the truth has been established, and I have no hesitation in pronouncing the sisters Rhoda and Cleoné to be of free condition."

Clitus now rose to address the court.

"I have an application to make that the proceedings in this case be annulled."

"On what ground?" said the Governor.

"On the ground that they were essentially illegal; that the evidence of the free-woman Rhoda was extorted from her by questioning that could not lawfully be applied."

"And you contend, therefore, that she should be set free?"

"That is my contention."

"And how about the woman Cleoné?"

"The question was embarrassing. Cleoné had suffered no actual wrong, and Clitus felt that here his case was weak. He tried to make the best of it.

"She has been treated as if she were of servile condition. The indictment against her is made out in these terms—'Also the slave-girl Cleoné,' are the words. I contend that it is informal, and ought therefore to be quashed."

The young advocate had the sympathies of the court—so far, at least, as the Governor was concerned—in his favour. He adjourned the court in order to consult his assessors. He found them adverse to the claim. A long argument ensued. In the end the opinion of the Governor prevailed, and he returned to the tribunal and began to deliver judgment.

"Having carefully considered the circumstances of this case, and remembering especially that the law, if ever it has been unwittingly betrayed into error, is anxious to make such amends as may be possible, I direct that the free women, Rhoda and Cleoné, wrongfully condemned as being of the servile condition——"

At this point the delivery of judgment was interrupted by the arrival of a messenger bearing an imperial rescript.

The Governor rose to receive the messenger, took the despatch from his hand, and, after making a gesture of respect to the document, proceeded to cut the sealed thread which fastened it. He read it, every one in court watching his face as he did so with intense interest.

It ran thus:—"Trajan Augustus, to his dearly beloved Cæcilius Plinius, Proprætor of Bithynia, greeting.—It is my pleasure that all persons, whether men or women, bond or free, who shall have been found guilty of cherishing the detestable superstition which has taken to itself the name of Christus, be forthwith sent to Ephesus, there to be held at the disposition of the Proconsul of Asia."

Every one knew what this meant, for the great show of wild beasts and gladiators that was about to be exhibited at Ephesus was the talk of the whole province.

15

THE AMPHITHEATRE

ALL Ephesus was on the tiptoe of expectation about the great spectacle that was soon to be exhibited in its amphitheatre. The preparations were on a scale of magnificence that exceeded anything that had within the memory of man been witnessed in the city. Several things had combined to bring about this result.

A wealthy merchant of Ephesus was going to expend two hundred thousand drachmas in gratitude to Diana, the great patroness of the city, for the preservation of his life. It was a vow that he had made when in imminent danger of shipwreck in the course of a voyage to Massilia, and he thought that he could not do better than fulfill it by giving a popular entertainment. The Roman Governor of Asia had added as much more. It was a handsome gift, but it may be doubted whether it represented a tenth part of what he had put in his pocket by the plunder of the provincials. But the Governor knew what he was about. There would be a chorus of a hundred thousand voices to praise his generosity, and he might reckon on its drowning a score or two of complaints about the extortion which he had practised and the bribes which he had received. Then the city had more than doubled the amount thus raised, by a vote from the municipal funds.

The Emperor had sent a present of money from his private purse, besides putting at the disposal of the managers of the spectacle a select troop of forty gladiators from his own establishment. The Prince's liberality found, as such liberality commonly does, many imitators. There were some especially notable gifts in the way of wild beasts; all parts of Lesser Asia of course contributed. There were panthers from Cappadocia, bears from Cilicia, and elks from Pontus. The Parthian king sent two magnificent lions and a tiger, and lent, for the purposes of the show, a troop of performing elephants, which he had himself hired at a vast expense from one of the princes on his Indian borders. Another Indian prince sent some curious apes which had cone from beyond the Ganges. There were even giraffes and ostriches from Africa.

Altogether, the show promised to be one of the greatest splendour, and the city was thronged with visitors from far and near. Among these were some connoisseurs, who were familiar with the splendid spectacles of the capital. And now a whisper went round that an exhibition of a peculiarly exciting kind was to be added to the usual entertainments. A number of persons who had been found guilty of holding the "odious superstition" of the Christians were to fight with wild beasts.

Public opinion was, indeed, not a little divided on this matter. Ephesus had not forgotten the venerable figure of St. John, and there were many, not themselves Christians, who regarded these cruelties with horror. Some had an intense curiosity to know whether the disciples would be rescued from their danger in the same marvellous way that was recorded of their teacher. On the other hand, there were many who looked forward to the promised exhibition with delight. These were bigots, not many in number, but very fervent and energetic, who sincerely hated all that threatened to undermine the old faith. And there was a multitude of people who, like Demetrius and his fellow-craftsmen some fifty years before, felt their livelihood to be endangered by the new belief. The silversmiths, who made models of the temple, or of the curious figure of the goddess herself; the less skilful artisans, who manufactured facsimiles of the meteoric stone, the "image which fell down from Jupiter," which had been an object of worship from times going back far beyond history; the bakers, who made a peculiar kind of cake stamped with the sacred image; the tavern and lodging-house keepers, who entertained and fleeced the pilgrims who crowded to pay their devotions at the shrine—all these looked upon the Christians as personal enemies. Lastly, the general population, though without any particular knowledge of or interest in the matter, regarded them with a vague suspicion as persons who threatened to diminish in some way the prestige of the great city of Ephesus.

The amphitheatre was a huge building, which must have contained—when closely packed, as we may be sure it was on the occasion about to be described—as many as thirty thousand spectators. The centre was occupied by the arena, in which the various spectacles were to be exhibited—a circular space, about two hundred yards in diameter, and covered with sand, from which substance, indeed, it got its name. Round it, tier upon tier, rose the seats of the spectators. These were divided into wedgelike portions, broad at the top, and tapering down to a comparatively narrow width at the bottom. The uppermost rows might have held about two hundred seats, the lowest something like five-and-twenty. A strong railing separated the lowest row from the arena. Between each two divisions there was a passage by which the various rows might be approached.

This railing, indeed, did not go round the whole circle. On the north side were ranged a number of enclosures, each with a strong door of its own, opening into the arena. From some of these the gladiators entered; in others the wild beasts that were intended for exhibition were kept. Others, again, served to hold the chariots before they started for a race. Above these receptacles was placed the seat of the Governor. His retinue and friends occupied other seats close by, and the notables of the city were placed at a greater or less distance, according to their rank. This was the aristocratic part of the amphitheatre, but generally the lower rows of seats were occupied by the more respectable class, while the upper were assigned to slaves and the lower class. A huge awning sheltered the whole of the audience from the sun or an occasional shower of rain. That part of it which was stretched over the seats of the Governor and the aristocratic company generally was of a rich purple. The effect of the sunlight falling through it was particularly striking.

The audience began to assemble as soon as it was light, for there was likely to be a crush for places; but it was about ten o'clock when the flourish of trumpets announced the arrival of the Governor. A small bodyguard of soldiers in the half-equipment usual on such occasions preceded him. His colleague of Bithynia, who had been specially invited to attend the spectacle, walked by his side. Next to him followed the Ephesian merchant who had contributed so liberally to the cost of the entertainment; and behind him came a long procession of the notabilities of the city, and then the "chiefs of Asia," local dignitaries of much importance, the priests of Diana, the town clerk of the city, the members of the Senate, and the officials of most of the chief towns of Western Asia Minor. The whole assembly rose to greet them, welcoming with special enthusiasm the great contributors to the entertainment. When all had resumed their seats, the Governor gave the signal for the proceedings of the day to commence.

The first part of the show was, we may say, ornamental. The ostriches, which had never been seen before in Ephesus, were especially admired. Yet greater applause was excited by some performing animals. A hunting leopard caught a deer, and brought it back unharmed. Still more astonishing, a wolf pursued and overtook a hare, and laid it uninjured at the feet of its trainer. But the palm was given by common consent to the troop of performing elephants. One animal traced the name of the Emperor in Greek letters with its trunk on the sand. Two others imitated a fight of gladiators with great skill. But most astonishing of all was the performance on the tight rope, when two of the animals carried a litter in which a companion, who represented a sick man, was lying. At midday there was an interval for refreshment, and the theatre became the scene of a gay and noisy picnic. The Governor delighted the people by his condescension in taking his meal in public. Every spectator was able to flatter himself with the social distinction of having lunched in the company of the chief magistrate.

The afternoon was devoted to exhibitions of agility and skill. Gymnasts lifted astonishing weights and made astonishing leaps, or constructed themselves into pyramids or other curious erections. Then there was fencing with foils and sword-play with staves, high leaping and long leaping, foot races, and quoit-throwing. It was the rule that there should be no bloodshed in the first day's performance; and the rule was not distasteful to a Greek audience. Greek feeling, indeed, was distinctly adverse to the cruel spectacles in which human life was so wantonly wasted. The more brutal taste of Rome had gone far to corrupt it, but the very best society at Ephesus, that which prided itself on a pure Greek descent, still held aloof from the theatre when these spectacles were going on.

However this may have been, there was no visible falling off in the attendance on the morning of the second day, and the interest was undoubtedly keener. A hundred pairs of gladiators contended during the day, and though this number was insignificant compared with what had been seen at Rome in the great Imperial shows, it was considered a more than respectable exhibition for a provincial city. During the early hours of the day there was little loss of life. The gladiators were always willing to disable rather than to kill an antagonist. They showed a forbearance which they hoped to have another day shown to themselves. And the spectators were unusually good-humoured. The weather was not too hot, and the awnings were admirably made to keep off the sun and admit the breeze. The Governor, too, by an arrangement with the tavern-keepers, had lowered the price of wine sold in the building, so that a quart could be bought for half a drachma.

Accordingly all went well; the wounded were permitted to escape with their lives, with the exception of an unlucky Thracian, who slipped where some blood had been spilt upon the sand, and spitted himself on his adversary's sword. But early in the afternoon an unfortunate mishap irritated the spectators. One of the most popular combats was that between a "netman" and a "fisherman," if we may so translate the classical names. The first was armed with a net and a trident, or three-pronged fork; the second had the ordinary weapons of a soldier. Zeno, the "netman," was a favourite with the Ephesians. He was a native of the city, he had fought for several years without ever suffering a defeat, and he was noted for the audacious agility with which he baffled his antagonists.

On this occasion he carried his tricks a little too far. He had already disabled three opponents, in each case bringing down roars of laughter by the comical way in which he made sport of his enemy —just as a matador makes sport of a bull. To put himself almost within reach of his sword; to elude him; to "net" him with a dexterous throw; and then, after dragging him, helplessly struggling in the folds, from one side of the arena to the other, to administer a disabling wound—had been the game which he had three times repeated, to the intense delight of his patrons. But the pitcher that goes often to the spring is broken in the end, and Zeno's fourth antagonist was his last. The man was a heavy, clumsy-looking fellow, and seemed to promise an easy victory. Deceived by his appearance, and elated by his previous successes, Zeno committed the fatal error of despising his enemy. He had thrown his net and missed his aim— that, of course, was a common occurrence: indeed, to finish the combat at the first encounter would have been held nothing less than a blunder. What the populace wanted to see was a victim gradually reduced to helplessness. Then he turned to fly. Here, commonly came in the best of the sport. To see the heavy-armed soldier toiling in vain after his light-footed antagonist; feeling him, time after time, almost within reach of his sword; sometimes striking out and missing him by little more than a hand's breadth (the dexterous netman often found the moment after the delivery of a fruitless stroke an excellent opportunity for a throw)—all this was a prime amusement to the crowd. But in this case the "fishman" was, though no one knew it, an athlete of uncommon strength. With a bound, of which no one would have thought a heavy-armed man to be capable, he leapt upon his antagonist, caught him by his girdle, and drove his sword into his back with such force that the point stood out under the ribs in front. Zeno fell almost instantaneously dead upon the ground.

A hoarse murmur of discontent ran round the benches. But the blow had been a fair one; in any other case it would have excited shouts of applause; and now it was impossible to find fault with it. Still, the people were profoundly irritated. When another pair of gladiators appeared in the arena, they were received with shouts of "Away! Away!" Then some one cried: "The Christians! The Christians!" and another voice answered with, "The lions! the lions!" The next moment the cries were blended into one—"The Christians to the lions!" and this was taken up with furious zeal by the whole assembly.

The Proconsul waited till the first rage of the outburst had been spent. Then he rose in his place.

"Men of Ephesus!" he said, in a voice raised to its utmost pitch, "you shall have your wish. But if you will listen to me, wait till tomorow. Now the day is too far spent."

At the same time he gave the signal for closing the entertainment, and the crowd, who knew that he meant what he said, dispersed in silence.

16

"THE CHRISTIANS TO THE LIONS"

SIXTEEN Christian prisoners in all had been sent from Nicæa to the great show at Ephesus. They were confined in cells, constructed under the seats of the amphitheatre, and indeed close to the cages of the wild beasts. That which was occupied by the two sisters, who, by special favour, were allowed to be together, was separated by nothing more than a wooden partition from the habitation of the lions. The heat, the darkness, and the stench were such as it would be impossible to describe. And if anything was wanted to aggravate the horror of the situation, the two prisoners heard day and night the restless pacing to and fro, and now and then the deep growling, of their ferocious neighbours.

Rhoda, indeed, was almost beyond suffering from these or any other causes. The journey to Ephesus had exhausted the scanty remnants of her strength, and since her arrival she had lain in an almost unconscious condition. All the noise of the amphitheatre had failed to rouse her, and even the fierce cry of "The Christians to the lions!" seemed not to reach her ears. Cleoné watched by her sister with the tenderest care. It was little indeed that she could do; but the beauty of the twins had touched the heart of the keeper of the beasts, and he had provided them with such little comforts as his means could furnish, the chief among them being a supply, often renewed, of fresh water from a well celebrated for its depth and coldness.

The first rays of dawn were just falling through the hole in the dungeon which admitted such light and air as were permitted to visit it, when, for the first time since her arrival, Rhoda seemed to rouse herself from her stupor. Cleoné, who, after a wakeful night, had fallen into a brief sleep, heard her move, and was immediately at her side. The sick girl turned a smiling face on her sister.

"I am going home to-day," she said.

"Yes, dearest," answered Cleoné, who had no difficulty in putting a meaning on her words.

"But you will stay," she went on.

"Nay, dearest, we will go together," said Cleoné, with a little tone of reproach in her voice.

"The Lord has not willed it so. You have something to do for Him here; but me He suffers to depart and be with Him; which," she added, after a pause, "is far better."

For a few minutes she was lost in thought. Then she threw her arms round her sister's neck, kissed her tenderly, and said: "You will marry Clitus, dearest?"

Cleoné, lost in astonishment, said nothing; she thought that her sister was wandering.

"I was wrong," Rhoda went on to say, "to hinder his love for you. Wives, too, have a vocation from the Lord. You will be not less faithful because you are happy."

"But, sister dear, you forget!" said Cleoné.

"No," returned the other, "I do not forget. But I have had a dream, and I know that the Lord showed me in it what shall be. This is what I saw. I dreamt that we two were walking together on a narrow road; and as we walked I saw two men in shining apparel who were talking together; and it was given to me to understand that they were two of the blessed Apostles, and that one, who seemed to be a man of middle age, and somewhat rugged and stern of look, was Peter; and the other, a youth of very fair and sweet countenance, was John. And Peter pointed to us two as we walked, and said to his companion, 'Brother, how shall it be with these two? Will they follow me or thee?' To whom answered John, 'One for thee, and one for me.' And it was given me to know that they to whom the Lord gives the crown of martyrdom are they that follow Peter, and that they who live long, and die after the common manner of men, follow John. For thus it was with these two when they were upon earth. And, lest I should doubt which of us two should live, and which should die, I dreamt again. And this time I saw you sitting with children standing by your knees; but the place where you were was wholly strange to me, and all the things about you such as I had never seen. Therefore I am sure that for you the Lord will shut the lions' mouths. And now, dearest, I would sleep again, that I may be ready when the time shall come."

Both sisters were resting peacefully when the keeper's wife entered their cell, about an hour after daybreak. She brought with her some food, which she had made as dainty as her means and skill permitted, and a pitcher of wine. Those doomed to death were commonly wont to dull their senses with heavy draughts of some intoxicating drink, and the kind woman was doing, as she thought, her best for the prisoners by giving them a liberal allowance. The sisters surprised her by begging for their usual supply of water from the well.

"Please yourselves," said the woman, "but I will leave the pitcher, in case you should think better of it when the time comes."

"Sister," said Rhoda, when they were left alone, "nothing need hinder us from remembering the Lord's death, according to His commandment, even though there be no minister to give us the bread and wine."

Cleoné gave a ready assent, and the two went through the simple ritual which St. Paul describes in his first letter to the Corinthians. This finished, they took their meal, which Rhoda ate with an appetite that she had not known for many weeks. All the time that was left to them they devoted to prayer. About nine o'clock the wife of the keeper of the beasts knocked at the door of the cell. She carried on her arm two white dresses.

"By special favour of the Governor," she said, "you are permitted to wear your usual clothing, and I have brought you these, for what you have is sadly soiled."

"The Lord reward you!" said the two sisters together.

The woman helped them to dress and arrange their hair, which, for want of a mirror (not part of the furniture of a prison), was sadly in disorder. She had just finished when the barrier that separated the cell from the arena was raised. One of the attendants of the amphitheatre beckoned them to come forward. Their companions had preceded them, and were standing in front of the Governor's seat. As the sisters, in obedience to the bidding of the attendant, moved across the arena to join them, there were visible and audible signs of emotion in the vast multitude that watched them. More pathetic figures could not have been seen than these two, as, hand in hand, with downcast eyes but unfaltering steps, they walked to their death. A ray of sunshine, falling through a chink in the awning, touched with a golden light the long tresses which fell over their shoulders. The angry cries which had greeted their fellow- victims were changed to a murmur of mingled admiration and pity. Not a few voices even raised a cry of "Pardon! pardon!" Had the Governor interposed to save them at that moment, not the sternest bigot for the old faith, not the most cruel frequenter of those hideous spectacles, would have questioned his action. But the multitude had not yet tasted blood; let them once have feasted their eyes on death, and innocence and beauty would plead for mercy in vain.

The condemned, after being thus exhibited, were put into an enclosure, from which they could be brought out one by one, or in pairs to be exposed to the fury of the wild beasts.

I shall not harrow the feelings of my readers by describing in detail the hideous scenes which followed. Each victim was provided with a weapon, a short sword or javelin, according to the animal which he was called upon to encounter. It was supposed that he fought with the beast, and the weapon was to give him a chance of victory—a chance that was a mere mockery, as scarcely even the most practised hunter could have used it to any purpose. Most dropped the weapon on the ground; one or two would have thought it sinful to use it. There was one exception, and this was the centurion Fabius, the officer whom my readers will remember as having commanded the arresting party on the occasion when the Christian assembly was surprised. Fabius had felt great remorse for the part which he had played on this occasion. The courage and faith of the prisoners whom he had been the unwilling instrument of taking had touched him to the heart, and he had resolved to make his long-delayed profession. Between the first and second hearing of the accused he had been secretly baptized, travelling to a neighbouring city for the purpose, and had then come forward and boldly avowed himself to be a Christian. He was now matched with a panther from Cappadocia, an animal of unusual size, which, in preparation for its duty as an executioner, had been kept in a state of starvation for several days.

The old fighting instincts of the soldier revived when the weapon was put into his hand, and though he did not hope or even wish for life, he resolved to strike a blow for himself. A pole stood in the centre of the arena, with the ground slightly rising round it. Fabius planted himself by this, with his short sword in his hand, and his eyes fixed on the panther as it crept cat-like towards him, waving its long tail backwards and forwards in its rage. His resolute attitude was greeted with a roar of applause from the spectators, who had viewed with contempt and disgust what they regarded as the cowardly submission of the other prisoners to their fate. When the panther had come within the length of its leap it paused awhile, dropping its eyes before the soldier's resolute gaze, but watching its opportunity. This was not long in coming. A puff of wind moved aside one of the edges of the awning, and sent a ray of sunshine into the soldier's face. For a moment he was dazzled, and at that moment, with a loud roar, the panther made his spring. Simultaneously, Fabius dropped upon his left knee, holding his sword firmly with both hands, as if it had been a pike. Had it been a more effective weapon, he might have escaped almost unharmed; as it was, the blade inflicted a long gash in the animal's breast, but bent, so poor was its temper, when it came into contact with the bone. Still, it checked the panther's attack, and the soldier was able to find a temporary shelter behind the pole. But the creature was not seriously wounded, and what was he to do without a weapon? The bent sword lay useless on the ground, and the beast was gathering its forces for another spring. Suddenly the soldier's eye seemed to be caught by something which he saw on one of the benches near the Proconsul's seat. He ran in this direction at the top of his speed, amidst a howl of disapprobation from the spectators, who thought this attempt at flight as cowardly as it was useless. But as he approached the side of the arena the reason for this strange movement became evident. A long hunting-knife, thrown by one of the spectators, came whirling through the air. An old comrade of the centurion's had bethought him of this as the only possible help that he could give. Fabius caught it dexterously by the hilt, and turned to face his savage antagonist. Man and beast closed in fierce encounter. More than once they rolled together on the sand. But the blade of the knife was of a better temper than the faithless sword. Again and again the soldier plunged it into the animal's side. In a few minutes he stood breathless, and bleeding from a score of deep scratches, but substantially unhurt, with the panther dead at his feet. A roar of applause, mingled with cries of "Pardon! pardon!" went up from the multitude.

The Governor beckoned the centurion to approach. "Well done, comrade!" he said. "The Emperor must not lose so brave a soldier. Hush!" he went on, perceiving that the centurion was about to speak, and fearing lest some ill- timed declaration of his faith might make it impossible to save him. "Hush! it is not a time to ask questions. A surgeon must look to your wounds; I will see you to-morrow." And the centurion was led out of the arena.

The turn of the two sisters was now come. Led to the centre of the arena, they sat down side by side awaiting their fate. Immediately the barrier of one of the dens was raised, and a huge lion bounded forth with a roar. It walked round the arena, and not a few of the spectators on the lowest tier trembled as he passed them even behind the stout iron railings which protected them. Of the two stationary figures in the centre the creature seemed to take no notice.

The spectators watched its movements with so fixed an attention that they scarcely noticed the darkness that had been for some time spreading over the building. A storm had been working up against the wind, and now broke, as it seemed, directly overhead. A vivid flash was followed by a deafening crash of thunder, and this again by a loud cry of dismay. The huge gilded eagle that stood over the Proconsul's seat had been struck, and came crashing to the ground, striking in its fall, and instantaneously killing, two of the Governor's attendants.

A thrill of fear was felt by the boldest and most philosophical spectator. As for the multitude, their superstitious terror rose to the pitch of agony. "The gods are angry!"—"Dismiss the assembly!"—"Let us depart!" were the cries that could be heard on all sides. The Governor rose in his place, and at the very moment of his rising the darkness seemed to roll away, and all eyes were turned again to the arena. Two white-robed figures were lying prostrate on the ground, clasped in each other's arms, and the lion was standing motionless by their side.

A few minutes afterwards, in obedience to the Proconsul's commands, the animal's keeper appeared. Several attendants accompanied him, for his errand was a dangerous one, and his best chance of safety was in being able to distract the creature's attention. As it turned out, nothing could have been more easily done. The lion seemed entirely to forget his hunger and his rage, and answering to the call of his name as readily as if he had been a dog, walked quietly back to his cage.

The sisters still lay motionless on the sand. The lion had not touched them, for there was not a trace of blood on their white robes; nor did it seem likely, so undisturbed were the two figures, that the lightning had struck them. But the attendants who had advanced to carry out the bodies readily perceived the truth. Rhoda was dead. Her strange revival on the morning of the day had been the last flash of an expiring fire. She had died, clasped in her sister's arms, without a struggle and without a pang. Cleoné had felt the heart cease to beat, and the cheek pressed against her own grow chill in death. Then her own sorrows were lost in a merciful unconsciousness. The spectators almost universally believed that the attendants were carrying away two corpses.

17

ESCAPE

CLITUS had watched the proceedings in the amphitheatre, not indeed from among the spectators, whose company would have been odious to him, but from the barred opening of one of the cages, which he had induced an attendant to allow him to occupy. As to what his course of action should be, he had been greatly perplexed. One thing only was clear to him: that he would not survive Cleoné. The law of his faith forbade suicide; yet surely, he thought to himself, it would not be difficult to die! He armed himself with a hunting-knife, though, of course, the idea of rescue was hopeless, and to use the weapon could only serve to provoke his own fate. Perhaps this was not very logical, if it was his duty not without necessity to endanger his own life; but much may be pardoned to a lover reduced to such desperate straits.

He had, as may easily be believed, never taken his eyes off the sisters. When, in the very crisis of the thunderstorm, he saw the lion approach them, he actually started from his hiding-place, and traversed half of the distance that separated them from him. When he saw them fall to the ground, some old story that he had read, of how the lion will not tear what he thinks to be a dead body, had come back to him, and this with such force that it seemed a message. He retraced his steps, and, so occupied was the audience with the storm, was unobserved both in coming and going.

He had since heard from the keeper's wife of the real fact about the sisters, and he had been anxiously considering what he could do. His hope, of course, was in Pliny. The Governor of Bithynia had treated him as a personal friend, and, though his conduct with regard to the Christians had not been consistent, it was clear that, on the whole, his leaning was to mercy. But how was he to be approached? He was the Proconsul's guest, and was probably now assisting at some state banquet, from which he could hardly be called. Yet time was short, and the need of taking some immediate action was urgent. He was walking up and down in front of the Proconsul's palace, deep in thought about his next step, when the problem was unexpectedly solved for him. A hand was laid upon his shoulder, and, turning to see who it was that wished to speak to him, he recognised the Governor's private secretary.

"Well met, most excellent Clitus!" was the young man's greeting. "I was just about to seek you at your lodgings. The Governor desires to see you without delay. Follow me!"

The secretary led the way to the Governor's apartment. Pliny was reclining on a couch. He was reading, for he never lost a moment that could be given to study; but he put down the volume when he heard the door open, and beckoned Clitus to approach. The secretary saluted, and withdrew.

The young Greek, who had not seen his patron close at hand for some time, was shocked at the change in his appearance. Occupied though he was with his own thoughts, he could not help remarking it. Pliny had the look of one who had not many days to live. He was beginning some expression of regret, when the Governor interrupted him.

"That matters not. I have more important things to speak of, and things that will not wait. But how did my secretary find you so soon? It is but just now that I sent him to fetch you."

"I had myself come, most Excellent, to the palace, in the hope of seeing you, but did not know how it was to be done. I thought you must be still at the Proconsul's table."

"Ah!" said Pliny, "I escaped from him. But not till I had got from him what I wanted. Look here!"

He took from a writing-case three documents sealed with the Proconsul's seal. He handed two of them to Clitus. They were orders addressed to the keeper of the prisoners, authorizing him to deliver up to the bearer the persons of Cleoné and the centurion Fabius.

"I had not much difficulty about the matter," said Pliny. "As to the girl Cleoné, I fancy that the way had been smoothed for me. The Proconsul has a heart, and possibly he might have let the girl go free after the wonderful deliverance of to-day; but her father has been with him, my secretary tells me, and, I fancy, gave him substantial reasons for pardoning her. He came yesterday, indeed, and offered three million sesterces for her and her sister's liberty; but then, of course, it was impossible. What he has paid now I do not know, but I feel sure that it was something large. However, this does not matter. There is the order for her release. As for the centurion, there was never any doubt. The Proconsul—you see, I speak freely to you—did not require any inducement here. He can admire a brave man without being bribed. So they are free. But the question is: Where can they go? Have you anything to suggest?"

"I thought of making my way into the Cilician Highlands," answered the young Greek.

" 'Tis a long journey to make, and a doubtful refuge after all. I have a better thought than that. There is a merchant of my acquaintance at Miletus who trades with Massilia and Britain. I have been able to do him some service, and he is anxious to repay me. Ever since I came I have cherished a hope of being able to do something for the prisoners, especially for the two sisters, whose case touched me more than I can say; indeed, but for this reason, I would have had nothing to do with this horrible spectacle. Well, I sent for my friend the merchant. He has a ship ready to sail, I believe, to-morrow morning. Get Cleoné and the centurion on board without delay: it should be done, if possible, before dawn to-morrow. I should say, Go as far as Britain. It is quite out of the world; no questions will be asked you there as to what you are or whence you come. But now there is another matter. Look at this!"

And he handed him the third of the three documents. It was an order for the delivery to the bearer of the body of Rhoda, lately a prisoner in the amphitheatre of Ephesus.

"There will be a difficulty here," Pliny continued; "I must leave you to overcome it. Cleoné, hard as it will be, must leave the care of her sister's funeral to others. To delay might be to ruin all. Unless you escape at once, there are some in this city who will take care that you do not escape at all. My advice is this. Take this document at once to the chiefs of your Society in Ephesus. Do it, I would say, before Cleoné knows anything about it. Let them remove the body. When it is gone, and not before, tell her. She will ask to see her sister before she goes. Then you must tell her. It will be a bitter pang to her; but she will see that it has been for the best. And now go—there is no time to lose; you have much to do before morning. The Proconsul has provided horses for your party, and an escort under an officer whom he can trust. And now for a few words for yourself. I shall never see you again; for my days, as I know well, are numbered. It seems a pity to banish so fine a scholar to an island of barbarians; but there is clearly no choice, and you can court the Muses there also. And then you will have your Cleoné. But you must not go penniless. I have arranged with my friend the merchant to hand you something wherewith you can start. That you may consider a loan, if you will, and repay to my estate. I shall not be alive to receive it. And I have put your name into my will; a legacy you can hardly choose but take. And now farewell! Remember me to Cleoné, and bid her not think too hardly of the Governor, though he was a pagan and an enemy of the faith."

"O my lord," broke in the young Athenian, eagerly, "it is not too late! There are those who will teach you; and if, as you say, you have but a few days to live——"

"I must make haste, you mean," said Pliny, with a faint smile. "Nay, my dear young friend, it is too late; or, rather, this faith of yours was never meant for me. It seems to make good men and women. I am sure that no one would die for the old gods as bravely and cheerfully as I have seen slaves and weak women die for their Christ. And you have a hope, too, I hear, of a life after death. It is a beautiful thought. I wish that I could have heard of it before. But now, you see, it is impossible. You will think of me, and pray for me. I hear that you do pray for others, even for those who hate you. Perhaps it will be well with me, after all; and, if not, I must bear it as I can, for I have tried to do my duty as a Roman and a man. But I must not keep you, or else our trouble will have been wasted. And now farewell!"

He reached his hand to Clitus. The young man would have kissed it, but Pliny drew him towards him, kissed him on both cheeks, and then laid both hands on his head. "My blessing on you," he said, "if the blessing of a heathen can avail. The gods, or, rather, the God, the Father whom we all acknowledge, protect you! And now, do not lose another moment."

It was a hard night's work that Clitus had to do. His first care was to see the Bishop of Ephesus. The good man willingly, or, it should rather be said, joyfully undertook the care of Rhoda's burial rites. One lock of her hair was taken as a remembrance for her sister. Then the body was removed by the bishop himself, with some helpers of assured loyalty, who might be trusted not to reveal the secret of her resting-place till the return, if such should be granted to the Church, of more peaceful times. The pious task was finished by the time, an hour after midnight, when Clitus presented himself at the house of the keeper of the amphitheatre, with the order of release in his hand.

In a few minutes Cleoné knew that she would never again see the outward form of the sister whom she loved, who was more than the half of her heart. But she had a faith, more vivid than is often granted to us, that the body is but the perishable image of the true man, and a hope of a future life, which the tribulations of the present intensified into an absolute assurance. And then she saw that the safety of her two companions, not to speak of herself, depended upon speedy action.

"You have done well," she said, after the first burst of grief was over, "and I trust you."

And she reached her hand to him, with a little smile that flashed for a moment through her tears.

The sun had scarcely risen when the good ship Centaur had cleared the harbour of Miletus and was speeding westward over the waters of the Ægean. Pliny, anxious to secure as far as was possible the party against disaster, had arranged with the captain to make the voyage to Britain direct, touching at as few ports as possible on the way, and these the most obscure. For some weeks after her embarkation, Cleoné was prostrated by illness—the natural consequence of all that she had endured. She was carefully and tenderly nursed by the captain's wife, for whose companionship the thoughtful care of Pliny had provided. Once or twice during her illness she seemed to herself to catch the tones of familiar voices; and several times, while she was slowly coming back to health, she saw figures which she seemed to know, and which appeared carefully to avoid her. It was not till after she had landed that the secret was revealed. It was her father and mother whom she had seen.

"Forgive him, for my sake," cried the poor woman, falling on her knees before her child; "you are all that he, that we, have left to us."

The old man stood two or three paces behind, his head bowed down with a shame and a remorse that passed all utterance. Cleoné threw her arms round his neck. Her tenderness divined that it was to him who had sinned that her love must first be shown. And the mother, to whom, by all laws of justice, that first embrace was due, was glad to have it so.

Lucilius had lost his son, who died the day after the removal of the sisters to Ephesus. Most of his property had been spent in purchasing the Proconsul's favour; with what remained he had determined to commence a new life in the land for which his daughter was bound. Clitus and Cleoné were married at the Christmas festival next after their arrival in the island, which, indeed, they did not reach till late in November. The next Easter Lucilius and his wife were baptized. Of the life of the family thus strangely brought together, little need be said, but that it was remarkably happy and prosperous. As the years went on, a little Bion and a little Rhoda recalled the sweet and tender memory of those who were sleeping far away under an Asian sky,—far away, but in that "sure and certain hope" which under all skies is still the same. Both were dear to their good neighbour Fabius, one of the senators of their little colony; but it was to Rhoda that the stout soldier- farmer would talk of one who had borne her name in days long past, best and most beautiful of women upon earth, and now bearing the martyr's palm before the Throne in heaven.

THE END